John Worthen

YOUNG FRIEDA

London
Jetstone
2019

Young Frieda by John Worthen.

A *Jet*stone paperback original.

ISBN 9781910858158

The right of John Worthen to be identified as author in this work has been asserted in accordance with the Copyright, Designs and Patents Act, 1988.

Cover design by The Ever Shifting Subject.

Author's Note

Young Frieda was conceived of and written as a *tête-bêche* (head to tail) novel starting from both ends, with its original cover looking like this:

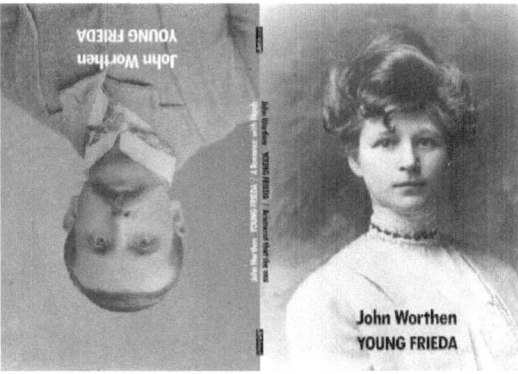

Between the two narratives an endless loop of explanatory text was designed to follow:

This loop can now be found following the end of the fictional memoir first printed. As reader, you are invited to start at the beginning of either memoir. Neither has priority; neither is designed to be read first.

Frieda Lawrence

"Aristocrat that she was"
by Frieda Lawrence geb. Freiin von Richthofen

A Memoir dictated by Frieda Lawrence
Ravagli, to be published after her death

" . . . completely at
peace and noble and
aristocrat that she
was."
(Joe Glasco, 16 August
1956)

El Prado, New Mexico
12 August 1954

To be myself is not always so easy. Sometimes I
lose myself in the past and it bowls me over. I
was seventy-five years old yesterday; now, sitting
up in bed as I do, every morning, with this lovely
girl Betsy beside me (ja, you must put that down)
taking dictation, I can tell what I now think is
the important story arising out of my past. One I
never told before. I shall be too old soon so now
or never. I would rather have it published when I
am dead, there are so many lies in the world.
  Two years ago I visited England and stayed with
my son Monty and one day he said "would you like
to see Ernest?" I must explain that he meant my
first husband, Ernst Weekley, whom I had left in
1912 and had not seen since the War (the first
War).
  We drove to the Putney house (Ernst lived there
with my daughter Elsa) and from the car window I
could even see the top of his head, in his study
(he was always working: Monty told me that he had
published a book only in January). There was very
little hair that I could see, but I knew the top
of that rounded head so well (under greying hair
in my time). It was strange.
  Monty urged me to go in, but on reflection I said
"no, after all I don't want to meet him". It
would have been a shocking meeting for us both,
and might have turned out terrible, I think. He
would perhaps have been upset, or angry, but I
know I would have been. I could feel my anger
just working up to the boil. I found at that
moment that I still hated him, just as I had hated
him forty years ago.
  I could not forget that for three whole years he
had denied me every chance of seeing my children,
and then limited me to occasional, half-hourly

visits. Without ever meaning to be away for more
than six weeks, I had last seen the children
properly when I left for the continent in 1912 –
and after such a long time the children had not
only in some ways forgotten me, but they had also
been subjected to a campaign of silence about me
(I learned that my name could never be spoken
aloud in their house, for example). They had also
been treated to propaganda (can I say that?) about
how lucky they were to have grand-parents and
aunts who were looking after them, in contrast
with their mother, who had gone off without them
and abandoned them.

When I first went away with Lawrence, I never for
a moment dreamed that I would not be seeing my
children again very shortly, or that Ernst would
not let me see them again, or that his family
would turn them against me. I thought that the
bond between mother and children was one which
nobody would dare to touch. Ernst believed that I
had broken the laws of men, but children in their
relationship to their mothers are another thing,
they are subject to a law of nature. I would
never have tried to break what was between him and
our children. He was however determined that my
immorality in leaving him had to be punished, and
his desire for revenge drove his actions.

When I sat in the car outside his house that
morning last year, all that he really was to me
was a bit of a man, as I saw him through the
window from the car parked in the street, reduced
by distance and distanced by panes of glass,
almost a nothing. But not nothing. He was still
the person who had hurt me so much, who had done
his best to destroy my relationship with my
children and had in that way altered the whole
course of my life.

While we were married, he had always seen me as
the desirable image of what he most wanted and
also believed in, and he had refused, so far as he
could, to know anything about the real me. I
believe he went on doing this for the whole time

2

we were married; so that in the end, not knowing
me, all he could do was hate me for leaving him,
and then take what revenge he could on me, doing
what would hurt me most. And in that way – not in
other ways – he succeeded.

I was also conscious of the oddest thing: that,
having exerted all his strength to prevent me
seeing my children, when I desperately wished to
see them, in old age he had ended up in the hands
of those same children who now badly wanted to
bring us together again . . . and I was now
turning down that chance, as firmly as he had
refused me my wish back in the old days. I rather
hope he never knew how close I had got to him in
his old age. I do however wonder if he ever
thought back to our time together. I guess he did
not: I was too far remote in the past, forty years
or so back, and he had done his best to kill me
off in his imagination, more than once.

In fact, I hope I was dead to him. I do not
forget the <u>verfaulte Leiche</u> (rotted corpse) which
he once described me as, in relation to the
children. I try to think of him with affection,
but I cannot. I don't think I can be fair to him.

But now he is dead himself. I heard the news
from England in May. Strange that his death
should matter so much to me. But when I heard
about it, it was as if I were hearing something I
had been waiting for ever since I left him. He
was old while I was still young, but what I wanted
from him was an end to his desire to revenge
himself on me. And that came only with his death.
I think I am glad he is dead.

I am, though, for certain glad that he died
before me, because it gives me the chance to go
over it all again, perhaps without the hatred.
Before, to talk about the intimate things of my
marriage would also not have been fair to the
living man, however much I hated him. I want to
say so many things he would have wanted kept
completely private; for example, the way I hope he
got something out of me as his young wife, before

I grieved him so much. I would like to see what I can say about those times now.

There is something else which helps bring all this back. My sister Else discovered some old diaries in Wolfratshausen and sent them to me; diaries which I wrote at times during my marriage, and one Tagebuch I kept when I went with Lawrence, and which also has poems in it, his best and most private poems to me, set down as he wrote them. That book helps me make sense today of that wonderful and also truly terrible time.

I caused Ernst such dreadful suffering. He could not bear the thought that I had left him for another man, although that is not exactly what happened. My daughter Barby said, however, that he was like a medieval Italian in feeling that he had been cuckolded. He thought he had been shown up as quite different from the man of the world which he always delighted to present himself as. Barby told me I ought to think of going back to him, after Lawrence had died. My only thought was "God help him then."

But I would like to describe how it was, before him but also with him. The children may be glad to have such an account. I have for years been filling notebooks with memories of my life as a child (I once promised myself: "I will write down all about myself and what happened to me") and I have also tried to write a fictional version of my life, calling myself Gisla, and managed some. But I had so many different ideas about how it should go! And so far all I have are fragments, many of them versions of very similar events in my childhood: the things I never forget, never can forget, and which I love to revisit in all their richness (all sun-drenched, that garden never changing) by writing them down. But they are not of so much interest to others, probably.

The story which is different, which I never wrote down before, is how I turned from a girl into a woman during the time I was married to Ernst, and had children with him, and while married to him

4

learned at last what love was and how I could love. And how my marriage ended. I never wrote down most of that story: just the start of it, and then a bit of the time with Otto (I am referring to the great Psychoanalytiker Otto Gross).

It must have shocked but I hope also a little amused Ernst when, after I had gone to Germany with Lawrence, I sent him some of Otto's letters to show what I now believed in. He (Ernst) would have been sensible enough to have known at once what optimistic nonsense those letters contained, for all their bright ideas about me and the future, in which Ernst would not have been so very interested.

That however was why what happened with Lawrence was so extracrdinary and in the end so terrible, when I lost my children: because having my children together with Lawrence would have been so right. I wanted both and could not see why I could not have both. Lawrence, though, thought that I had to choose between him and them. I disagreed and we quarreled about that, even very early on.

It would have been terribly difficult, and how we would have managed with money, I do not know, though Lawrence was the kind of person who always solved our money problems, one way or another.

But Lawrence did not want my children, he made that very clear, and for the moment, anyway, when we were first together, all he wanted was to find a good place to live where he could also write, in order to earn for us. Ernst would have hated the thought of his children being influenced by someone he despised as much as he despised Lawrence. So the two men, without knowing it, collaborated in keeping my children from me.

That is encugh preliminary talk. Now I must embark on my first chapter! Betsy - please -

I can begin with all the names and titles I ever had. Mrs. Emma Maria Frieda Johanna Freiin von Richthofen Weekley Lawrence Ravagli. That says a lot already.

I was born the daughter of a Baron so had the title "Freiin von Richthofen". I have been married three times, hence the names of my three husbands. My parents gave me four first names, I don't know why; perhaps they were not sure what to call me. But Frieda or Friedele was what I was mostly called. (Lawrence used Johanna for me in his writing, several times.)

My parents were loving at first, my mother told me, but they quarreled horribly. There was an occasion when I was about fifteen and which my sister Else told me about, when my father did not come home at night, and in the morning my mother sent our faithful manservant Wilhelm to look for "the Herr Baron" in the town. At eleven o'clock he appeared; Else said he was white, shaking, a pitiable sight. He had been invited to the casino by some soldier colleagues, had gambled there, and had lost a huge sum of money. "I'll blow my brains out and have done with it!" he swore. My mother Anna, said Else, was very angry, and told him not to dare do such a thing: he had children to care for. So he insisted to my mother that they go to a lawyer to take out a mortgage on the Sablon house to raise the money, and she had protested: "That money belongs to the children. You want to take their money to pay your gambling debts with." But in the end she went to the lawyer and signed, still protesting: "I stay with you in the house for the children's sake, but I'm your wife no more." And that had been the end of their marriage in all but name; they hated each other. And we lost the ownership of the house and garden I loved so much, and in the end we had to move out, again I think because of my father's debts. He still owed a thousand Marks (about two thousand dollars, I believe) when he died.

Else knew more than I did, but even I knew I had to be two different people. I had to be my father's adored girl, teased and loved, even if forbidden at times. But I had to be my mother's daughter too, one who had no time for her father. It was hard, not taking sides.

It was as I grew up that I knew that I had to leave home as soon as I was able. My sister Else felt the same, and by qualifying herself at her university had already prepared the way for her leaving. My younger sister Johanna, usually called Nusch, simply wanted to get married. It was terribly distressing. It tore me in half.

I had been born in Metz in 1879. The Richthofens
had been landowners and administrators in the far
east of Germany, in Silesia (now Poland) ever
since the family came into existence: the very
first Richthofen, Johann Praetorius (1611-64) was
my own great-great-great-grandfather. He had
taken his title on being raised to the Bohemian
knighthood. (I must here thank Betsy's husband
Richard for digging out all these dates and
references for me.)

In the German baronial system, with the title
passing on to all the sons, Richthofens soon
spread all over Germany; but my sister Else told
me that the problem for our particular branch of
the family arose in the mid-nineteenth-century,
during the lifetime of our grandfather Ludwig, who
"lost somehow his possessions" in the highlands
and backwoods of Upper Silesia, where (following
his father) he had become a Landrat - district
administrator - for various neighborhoods and had
married into the Polish-German aristocracy (his
wife was a von Laschowski, whose mother had been a
von Skrbensky: I told Lawrence about all this, and
her name got into The Rainbow).

By the mid 1840s the family was living at
Raschowa near Koesel in what my father called "a
small castle with a small lake". But - presumably
because of their debts - they had to abandon the
castle (which no longer exists), and my
grandfather Ludwig himself, in old age, after the
death of his wife, lived with his daughter Helene
and her husband Emanuel Langer at Szczerbice, down
to the south east of Koesel. The family's
property - its small castle - was now gone.

My father Friedrich von Richthofen had been born
on 29 July 1845 but - like his sister and brother
- had ended up with "no foothold" in Silesia: they
were the first of their family to be without any
land of their own. The family's surviving male
children had to branch out in new directions and
take up careers. My father's elder brother

(another Ludwig) became a lawyer and went into the
civil Prussian government, while my father, the
only other son to survive childhood, joined the
Prussian army as an officer cadet at the age of
seventeen, in 1862. I have a photograph of him
with the other officer cadets, in his uniform: he
looks small, broad-faced, handsome and determined.
By August 1870 he was fighting in the Franco-
Prussian war of 1870-71; and by January 1871 he
had risen to the rank of Oberleutnant (second in
command to the captain of his regiment).

He kept a diary of the campaign which I later
translated; it runs from the fighting which
started around Strasbourg, down to a couple of
days before he was wounded in the hand by a
bursting mortar-shell in January 1871. This was
the defining moment of his whole life. He was
apparently briefly taken prisoner by the French
and treated by a French doctor, but was soon back
in German hands, at the hospital in Karlsruhe.
His right hand had been permanently damaged,
however, and the wound put an end to his career as
an active soldier. On his big writing desk
thereafter lay not just the usual paraphernalia of
sealing wax and seal and pencils (all neatly
sharpened) but broken shell splinters on a
malachite base. I once asked him what these odd
things were and he told me. He kept the actual
evidence of what had wrecked his career.

Because of his injury, he was discharged from
active service on 2 October 1871 with a war
pension, the rank of lieutenant and the Iron
Cross. A photograph of him which I think Else has
shows him bandaged, decorated and defiant but in
civilian clothes. Another photograph shows him
glaring at the camera, firing himself into it,
eyes blazing, in standard Prussian fashion. "Er
scheint streng, aber er war es nicht", my sister
Else once said; he looks stern but he wasn't. She
said it with tenderness; we sisters all had a
tender condescension for men, which began with
what we felt for our father (it was in the end

what I felt most strongly for Lawrence, too).

My father made his new, desk-bound career in the renamed and now German region of Elsass-Lothringen, with a succession of jobs in the military administrations of the conquered and occupied cities. This was how he remained in the army after his injury.

It was in Konstanz, however, that he got married, in 1872. Family legend insists that it was during a visit by the Kaiser Wilhelm I to Konstanz that my father observed a young woman presenting flowers to the Kaiser and got into conversation with her. She was Anna Marquier, daughter of the lawyer Adolf Marquier; she was six years younger than my father and would marry him just after her own twenty-first birthday.

She had been born in Donaueschingen, at the source of the Danube, high up in the Black Forest, and in the 1850s still utterly isolated; its only regular contact with the world being the stage-coach that arrived at nine at night, with newspapers and letters. There was one grocery shop, and pedlars still served the community. The Marquiers sensibly got their children educated in more thriving places. My mother was sent to the nearest center of civilization, Freiburg, to be taught by the sisters Julie and Camille Blas in Littenweiler.

After marrying my father, my mother and he moved to a post he had acquired in the engineer's department of the administration in Château-Salins, and it was here that their first child was born, my sister Else. By the late 1870s, they had moved again, for my father to take up a more responsible post in the engineers' department of the administration in Metz, as an Imperial construction supervisor (kaiserlicher Baurat: it always sounded so splendid, though it was still just a desk job); and it was here that my mother had her two other children. I was born in 1879 and Nusch I think in 1883.

But this was a problem. My uncle Ludwig's

marriage had produced only a daughter, and my father had only daughters from his marriage; so our particular branch of the Richthofens died out in our generation. This was the second reason (after his war wound) for my father to grow disappointed. Without a son to succeed him, he lost his faith in himself, he lost faith in everything - for as he grew older increasingly he gambled, womanized, quarreled horribly with our mother, dearly loved us but always tried to impose his will on us too.

He seems only to have been thoroughly happy when away from home, out hunting with the local French nobility, living the aristocratic life which he mourned and to the loss of which he could never be reconciled.

I once read in a book an account of him spending much of his life depressed, "pining for the gentleman farmer's existence that had been his birthright". If you had told my father that he was pining to be a "gentleman farmer", he would have knocked you down. A farmer indeed! A gentleman only! He was a nobleman: he had been born and brought up in a castle.

I in my turn grew up accepting, as very important, what my sister Else always ironically referred to as the importance of the Richthofens in a "romantic" way. I don't think it was romantic. On the contrary, my feeling that I am a Richthofen helps me account for my feeling of difference (underline that, please) from other people. Otto saw this and felt it (he once alluded directly to my "sichere selbstverstaendlich Adelsherrschaft", my "confident natural aristocracy"), as did Lawrence, and Maria and Aldous Huxley too. Ernst never did.

And even if thinking back to my own aristocratic status and nature is a kind of self-indulgence, it has nevertheless always had significant consequences for me. I never forget how the young Ida Wilhelmy, the children's nurse, reacted to me when I first understood how pale and ill she was,

working for that German Jewish family, the
Flersheims, in Nottingham: and she so young! She
had come over to us with the Flersheims' daughter
and their new grand-daughter, but was so obviously
ill that I insisted she was put to bed at once, in
our house, and got Dr Stafford in to see her. I
just took control: and when eventually she got
better, she simply stayed with us, and we started
to pay her wages: "after all, one often felt the
'Baroness' very strongly!" Ida remembered. I was
young then, but I do not think I have changed
much.

When I was two, my family moved from its flat in the city of Metz to the house in Sablon with the large garden, on the edge of the country. (I think that the death of my paternal grandfather, at the age of 80, may have led to his children inheriting whatever oddments were left of the von Richthofen money, and thus making the move possible.) From my descriptions of it to him, Lawrence produced a word-painting of the Sablon house: "The Baron's house stood square and grey in its big garden, among the fields. Across, the low swarm of the barrack's buildings." The proximity of the house to the soldiers' barracks was actually the most striking thing about it. (A satirical friend once sent us a postcard addressed simply to "Sablon Metz / Swamp behind the barracks".) We only moved out of this house on Route d'Augny when I was seventeen. It was the house of my childhood, and became the setting for many of my memoirs, because I always felt I belonged so passionately to it and its gardens. I quickly forgot the fact that I lived at another address for my last years at home; but that, anyway, was when I was a plump teen-ager, spending a lot of time down in Littenweiler, being educated like my mother by the Blas sisters.

As adolescents in Metz, however, we young Richthofens were naturally most aware of the junior officers, those we could dance with! But as children we had been constantly aware of the ordinary soldiers in their barracks so close to us. We learned the songs they sang; and, for example, in Christmas week Nusch and I received invitations from the Bavarian soldiers who lived in temporary quarters near our house. On the soldiers' Christmas tree hung sausages and cigars; we brought them biscuits and the soldiers carved little wooden animals for us.

We also played hide-and-seek in the trenches the soldiers dug in the fortifications, and there we had to dodge the sentinels; we got terribly hot

and dusty racing around all afternoon in the huts
and foxholes.

And I never forget the wisteria climbing up and
over the balcony of our house, my bedroom with the
flowered chintz, the painted clock on the landing
outside; the love, the feeling of my parents,
figures in my childhood of more than life-size,
all the happenings, so exciting to a child, every
happening a mystery, a wonder. I am glad I had
this. It was freedom, though it was also
privilege, as I came to realize.

All my own memoirs recreate this period in my
life with especial love and care, even when
describing my quarrels with my elder sister Else,
who had no time for dreams of aristocracy but
insisted even as a child that her own and her
siblings' pocket money should be docked in order
to buy Christmas presents for the family of our
washer-woman, Frau Seidel. We sisters grumbled
but we allowed it to happen: Else was too potent a
force in our young lives.

Else grew up with a profound social conscience;
she also struggled with immense determination
against our father's disbelief in education for
girls, and eventually overcame his opposition to
her going to University. She studied economics,
and pursued her interests in the lives of the poor
and disadvantaged.

My younger sister, Nusch, was the absolute
opposite; always spoiled, exceptionally beautiful,
growing up admired by everybody, even more focused
on balls and young men than I was, but taking life
as she found it. I was the tomboy, climbing
trees, getting bad reports at school, being called
an "Atavismus" (something demonstrating a strange
recurrence to a primitive past) by my mother, but
in particular loving my father: his habits, his
room with its dogs, his hunting trophies and
plants, his tenderness towards me. I thought him
perfection on earth. I wrote and rewrote the same
series of reminiscences of him; how he was a
lovely father who composed poems for me when I was

small: how I must have all the virtues of the
animals, quick as a bird and gentle as a lamb, and
busy as a bee, "and gay as a Spitz, be my little
Fitz", his poem ended. He must also have read
Prescott's Conquest of Mexico at one time and had
such names as "Fitzli-Putzli" for me. When I was
about six he took me to the Officer's swimming
establishment and dived into the Moselle with me
from the diving-board, that taught me to swim, and
much to the astonishment of the officers I emerged
dressed in my small girl's clothes. In another
piece of writing I recalled "the surprise of being
under water, but I emerged and swam around like a
tadpole. After that I could swim." That sounds
just like me – and not just after my sudden
immersion in the Mosel, either, but when I emerged
in other places too, and found I could cope, and
more than cope.

At quite a late stage, shortly before I left
home, it however became clear to us sisters that
our father had somewhere a mistress called Selma,
who was milking him for money, and who around 1896
had had a child, a son who later died and who may
have been my father's; we never knew. What we did
know was that our parents' marriage was violently
quarrelsome, full of hatred for each other. The
fact that we three daughters all left home so
early showed our determination to get away. Our
father's debts meant that we lost the Sablon house
when I was seventeen, and moved into a flat in
Montigny; but I said that.

I can also say that my childhood was something
that in my own way I have never lost: the
sensation of being a child in a wonderful world
where I feel free and happy. I have consciously
re-created that world all my life, not just in my
reminiscent writings but so far as possible in the
way I have lived. With Lawrence, I managed it all
the time, as when we set off to walk over the
Alps, and walked for six weeks, stopping where we
liked, sleeping in hay huts! And when we lived
beside the sea in Fiascherino; and then in

America, when we were rebuilding the ranch, and we slept out of doors up on the hillside, under the stars. And sitting up in bed like this, and talking, I feel once again like a child. This is what our old age brings back to us.

My happiest memories of those days after we left the Sablon house, and before I married, were at the Eichberg house, in Littenweiler. This was why sometimes I called myself "Eichfried": it was the place which I felt had become part of me, and to which I went whenever I could. I remember a seat in the garden at the Eichberg house, high up on the hillside, so that one saw right out across the country, and just the roof of the house below; one of those nice benches built around a tree (a cherry, in this case).

This was a place I had discovered when I was a pupil at the Maedchenpensionat and where I went with my best friends and we all sat round together: the blossom on the trees was wonderful in the spring. The view became my favorite view in the world; the house took the place of my family home when I was away from it and after we lost the Sablon house I went on loving the Eichberg house and the land around it.

I took Ernst up there one day – the day that his friend Professor Schröer had a camera with him – with the house dog; and though the day was rainy, and I was wearing my new dark grey dress, Ernst asked me to take my pink and white sun hat with me, as he always loved to see me in it. And Professor Schröer took a photograph of us there in which my sun hat makes me look like a young nun. Ernst always loved that picture. I hated it. I never felt like a nun, however much I might have looked like one.

It was however a sign that Ernst wanted me then as a man wishes for a pure woman: I was so young, so pure, he believed! I wanted, myself, to be as I always had been, not always pure.

I saw the place just once more. Aunt Julie had died (this was after the War), but great-aunt

Camille was still there, almost unchanged she
seemed. I went to Littenweiler from Freiburg for
the first time by train, with Else and Nusch, and
with Lawrence too, who did not really want to
come. But I put our names in Camille's old
visitors' book and could not resist turning back
the pages to 1898 and seeing Ernst's name there
too . . . and I walked up to the old cherry tree
and seat, and looked out, as ever. It was still a
special place, though Littenweiler was growing in
all directions, and houses were spreading up along
the Eichbergstrasse. I never knew what happened
either to Aunt Camille or to the Pensionat; both
long gone now, I guess.

4

How did I get married? That is the question I
have asked myself over and over. I know that at
the age of eighteen I had the fantasy of a simple,
strong, handsome man, almost certainly a soldier,
who would carry me off from my home life. I also
remember that in the middle of June 1898, just
before my nineteenth birthday, I had two boy-
friends, both soldiers, and both of whom very much
wanted to marry me; and I had actually agreed to
get married to one of them.

This was to Kurt von Monbart, whom I had known
since I was seventeen. He was seven years older
than me and I had never even kissed him but he
fascinated me; he had an unforgettable voice and I
thought of him as my soul mate. I was determined
to marry him if he was able to do what I wanted
him to do, which was to resign his commission and
start a job which would support us. I believed
that he would do this: I was well aware that
neither of us had enough money on which to live if
he tried, as a married man, to continue with a
military career. But I was also going to help
support him; I too would work if that proved
necessary. I had promised him this.

It felt like a new start, and I told Else about
what I hoped for (Monbart and I had at times
communicated via her: she called him "the stern
one"). And I hoped we would have children, and
carry on the Monbart family name, which I had
always loved.

But then I went down for some weeks as usual in
the summer with my parents to stay with the Blas
sisters, in Littenweiler; and one hot day in July,
up near my favorite tree and seat I saw two men
coming towards me. One was Professor Schröer,
whom I had never liked very much (I liked his wife
much more: he was only ever an academic, in all
moods). The other man was a tall handsome man
with drooping mustaches whom I did not know. He
took his hat off to greet me but then kept it off,
as if mesmerized by me, and I found it hard to

take my eyes off him. I had encountered Ernst
Weekley, a compelling Englishman and also a
Professor with so much of what Max always called
charisma, and so handsome - and, as I quickly
learned, so dependable, so hard-working, so
supportive - who (he told me soon afterwards) fell
in love with me immediately. He was quite
different from the German professors I had met,
especially in Freiburg, who (like Professor
Schröer) were always a bit pompous and full of
themselves. This one seemed simply
straightforward, if a bit shy, but he smiled so
nicely!

Of course I wanted love, though I knew nothing
about it. But now everything I had wanted
suddenly seemed to fall into my lap all at once.
Ernst got permission from my father to see me on
my own and we arranged to meet by the fountain in
the woods the next day or just soon after, I
forget.

But the memory of what it was like is still very
powerful for me. I remember how excited I got as
I neared the place. I was intensely conscious of
my pink and white frock, with the pink and white
sunbonnet which I had put on because he had told
me he loved it. But it is also true and probably
significant that I thought more of my effect on
him than of himself. At last I saw him standing
in the entrance of a somber pinewood, the trees
forming a deep archway behind him.

At this point in our Freiburg time he was like a
man lifted out of ordinary life. I imagine him to
be someone who felt that he was nothing by
himself, that his sole being was in my
approaching. It was rather frightening: it felt
as if his emotion were paralyzing him.

It made me thoroughly uncomfortable; I went up
to him. He took me in his arms for the first
time. But he did it gently, tenderly, I knew he
was repressing his passion so far as he could, so
as not to frighten me. "My sunflower", he said.
His eyes were so reliable, dog's eyes they were,

honest brown eyes. And how he worshiped me. I loved it. But also I didn't love it.

However, we announced our engagement in Littenweiler a couple of weeks later, on my nineteenth birthday.

Sometimes to start with Ernst did frighten me, though not with the strength of his passion. I felt once again uncomfortable when, in a fit of reverence, he kissed my feet, which seemed to me rather large, ordinary feet in not too elegant boots. It flattered my vanity, and I accepted it as the behavior of a man in love. But I did not think better of him because of it.

Dimly, I knew that he was in love with an ideal, not with me, and that I really was not this ideal person whom he loved. But I also resolved to live up to his ideal love, to be as it were the sampler of all the virtues he thought me possessed of. For him I would be perfect.

So I wrote to Monbart, telling him that I was engaged to another man and in love with him too; I knew that was the right thing to say, though I didn't actually know what it meant. It felt a very brutal thing to write to someone who had proposed marriage to me, and whom I had accepted, and who was I was sure in love with me, but it was the only honest thing to do, though it was also the burning of a bridge, or a boat.

I know I had to leave Freiburg shortly afterwards. We must have said goodbye at some point, but I don't remember it. Ernst was in Bern for a bit, and then he came back to see me in Metz, and we were able to spend a few more days together, visiting my friends there and proudly telling them what had happened. What I do remember are the letters that came from him when he had finally returned to England; yards of them, in almost perfect German – better German than mine, certainly. He told me over and over how much he loved me, how much he longed for me. I was impressed, but also wondered what I should be feeling when I read them. Whatever it was, it seemed, at any rate, a good deal less than what he himself felt.

I told myself, however, that when we were married, then I would start to feel love like his. For the moment, I simply told Else and Nusch that he was in love with me and I had accepted him; and they congratulated me and both found him very handsome.

I was so profoundly ignorant of everything; I am astonished when I look back, how naïve I was about men, and marriage, and about my future in a foreign country.

The next thing I remember is his arriving in Germany in December, to take me and my mother to England, to meet his family (it was now, I think, that he gave me my engagement ring which sadly I lost, many years ago). We caught the train to Calais, and then found ourselves on a small boat tossing about on the way to Dover.

I confess that at this point my heart sank; crossing over to another country, in such bleak weather, I felt as if I were going into exile. I wanted to cry. "Don't be a goose", whispered my mother, who could see what I was starting to feel. I was wearing my sailor dress, with a cap, which had seemed so appropriate.

Ernst took good care of my mother too: "Look, Mama", he said, "now you can see the cliffs of old England." There, out of the white vapor, rose a concrete whiteness, the Dover cliffs. And his parents were there: she amazingly round and very cheerful, talking all the time (I could understand almost nothing she said), his father very upright and white-bearded, reserved but kind, as I learned.

Ernst helped me by translating what his mother was saying; she never really realized that being foreign meant that I could not follow all that she said. We left my mother in Dover and went to their tiny house in Hampstead, filled with their children (Ernst was the eldest of nine). I think I was the only person in the house awarded a room of my own!

We went to church on Christmas Day, all dressed up specially; and the church was so different from the Garnison church in Metz, where all the men stood and sang, so loud and firm. Here in Hampstead the women were louder than the men: and the men kneeled, which the officers in Metz had never done. They all seemed such good people, I wondered why they needed to pray or go to church.

In theory I was there to decide whether I could bear getting married to an Englishman, and living in England, but everything seemed entirely taken for granted; we discussed our plans for the wedding (or rather everything was explained to me), for example how Ernst's brother Bruce (a smiling pastor, who was there for Christmas) would conduct the service. Ernst proudly wanted to show me his house in Nottingham, but there was no time to go; my mother was still waiting for me down in Dover!

When we went back down to Dover, we were accompanied by Ernst's sister Maude, who did her very best to be nice to me; but it was clearly an effort. She made me feel very young and very silly. She was also dressed so badly in comparison to me, and commented all the time on my clothes and how expensive they must be. That night in Dover, when Maude and Ernst had gone back, my mother asked me how it had really been, and I told her that everyone had been very kind, and took for granted that I would be marrying; and my main problem was the English language! At no point did I ask myself whether I really wanted to get married to this man, or move to England; I was in a kind of trance in which I only attended to dates and times and arrangements, and never to any of my feelings.

And so my mother and I went back, I must say a little sadly on my part, to our silent and often distressed and angry home in Metz. The kindness and generosity of the Weekley family seemed to radiate through their little house. That was

almost the only thing which made me feel I was
right to get married; there seemed so much human
warmth in England.

The summer following, we got married, down in
Freiburg, where I had always been so happy.
Although he was an Englishman, and my father had
warned us against marrying foreigners, my parents
were very happy that he had chosen me. The only
one of the family who did not seem so happy was
Else. She had said she thought that he was an
academic hysteric who repressed everything. But
she always saw people in this Freudian kind of
way. And even she was impressed by his love for
me.

I don't remember much about the wedding except
for something that happened that morning, when
Ernst and I were waiting for my family to get
ready to go to the church. We were both dressed
up, but he kneeled down, in his wedding suit, and
his wing collar, saying "With God's help, I will
make your life happy. I will live for that and
for nothing else". And him so handsome, with his
charm, and his wide-open, almost staring brown
eyes, and the beautiful line of his brow. At the
time I found it wonderful, now I ask myself how it
was possible, him on his knees, with his heels up,
how I could ever have believed him so wonderful.

My wedding ring I gave to Katherine when I
married Lawrence and she and Jack Murry were our
witnesses.

Over the years I have written and given to people
at least two accounts of my wedding night, with
very different conclusions. In one, I stand
suicidally on the hotel balcony after Ernst has
made love to me (and has fallen asleep), feeling
cheapened and exploited, disgusted at what has
been done to me, but also telling myself that only
chambermaids jump from balconies. But in another
account I feel nothing but surprise that this
moment, made so much of by poets, should have felt
so unimportant. Both are true. And it was never
so bad again as it was that night. It was really
a rape, as I understood later. He hurt me and

then hurt me again, and I protested but he never stopped until he had finished. I was as much disgusted with it all as actually hurt by him.

I am sorry Betsy but you must accept all the sex there is going to be in the course of my talking! It will get worse! Yes, keep that in!

But all I can say is that after what happened that first night in Luzern, I never really wanted him, though I accepted him when he wanted me. For him it was always a matter of his achieving his own pleasure, having his orgasms, as I learned they were (I knew nothing about them when I got married), as often as he could, and then retreating to his own side of the bed, or to his own room when we slept separately. He never said anything to me; if anything, he seemed a little embarrassed at doing what he did. He very rarely aroused me, and then only by accident. I enjoyed it, when that happened, but I did not know quite how it happened. And he never made me feel wonderful. He treated me, really, as a pleasant way of making babies. I put a stop to that after Barby. And sex for him never seemed more than a kind of emptying of himself into me. That was my final conclusion. But I didn't know it could be different. I assumed that the poets of sexual love were liars. It would not have been the first time; and they were nearly all male poets, too.

Life in Nottingham, when we finally got there, was much harder than I had thought it would be. The house, so much looked-forward to, depressed me the moment I went into it; it was much smaller than I had imagined, and so dark (one of those houses which only gets in light in the front, and then again right at the back, so that the hallway and the stairs are dark, even on a bright day, unless one puts on the gas; and even then came the curious indescribable smell of somewhere sunless). Really, Ernst had tricked me into thinking it was a large house, though perhaps it was from his point of view. When I unpacked our wedding presents and set them up on the dresser, old Bohemian glass and old silver, and put down my beautiful rugs, they all looked so forlorn in that house.

About twenty years ago I wrote a few paragraphs about our life in this house, before Monty's birth. This is what I wrote: Betsy, the notebook is on the floor beside you.

                    *   *   *

"The only room I loved was Ernst's study; the walls were books, the whole room seemed books, books on the writing-table, books on the floor. And then the smell of his pipe, it was so evidently a man's room, his room, I liked it. I would throw myself down on the hearthrug with a novel, one side of me baking comfortably at the fire. Those evenings when the children were asleep and he was lecturing were a treat to me.

I would get utterly absorbed in my novel before he came in, tired to death after his two evening lectures. He would run up the stairs; his face was white with exhaustion, his eyes brilliant with his effort. A wave of tenderness would rise in me at sight of him, so tired, working so hard, so uncomplainingly for the children and me. The maid brought a plate of soup for him on a tray. He gave me a look and sat down eating it, the spoon so neatly held in his beautiful hand."

*   *   *

I tried to be accurate when I wrote that, but what
I did not think it right to say was that the
tenderness (please underline that) was all I ever
felt for him. Where another young wife would have
felt she loved him, I never could or did. I did
admire his hand, it was beautiful, but I never
wanted it to caress me. That now seems to me sad,
but that was how it was, and other things carried
me along. More quotation!

*   *   *

"'I am a damned good lecturer', he said, wiping
his drooping mustache with his napkin, shaking his
head proudly.
   I admired him then, when he exulted in his work."

*   *   *

Yes, I admired him for his work, but he seemed so
self-contained, with his books and his writing. I
came second, such a long way behind. All I could
find that really absorbed me were the novels I
constantly read. He sometimes noticed this:

*   *   *

"'You condescend to speak to me tonight', he
said. 'Yesterday you were so absorbed in your
book that you did not answer my questions except
with an occasional grunt.'
   'Sorry', I said, 'is it as bad as that? Lord,
but this is exciting. I love Stendhal.'
   'He is supposed to be something wonderful', he
answered.
   'I don't care a twopenny damn what he is supposed
to be', I burst out, 'but I have not read anything
that's got hold of me like this "Le Rouge et le
Noir".'
   'I daresay, it's the kind of modern stuff you
like', he said, 'with your Nietzsches and
Platos'."

*   *   *

Now a lot of that is simply bad invention. Ernst
had read everything, everything, including (of
course) French literature: he was a Professor of
French! And he had actually brought me books to

read like "Le Rouge et le Noir" and asked me what
I thought of them. But he would never (either)
have said that Stendhal was "modern stuff". Zola,
perhaps, and Nietzsche. But equally certainly not
Plato as modern!

I am not sure, either, that I would ever have
said "I don't care a twopenny damn". That is
exactly Ernst's way of speaking, his sort of
knowing slang. One learns one's language from
one's partner, but we spoke German together at
home, always, and I don't think this is very
convincing as German either.

I find I cannot trust many of these early
memories, now I look at them again after so long.
I think I had decided that I would write it all
out as fiction, so I put bits of fiction in, which
now come over as if they were facts. The only bit
I now remember to be certainly true is the way I
remember "when I had my Plato fit on and I began
at breakfast, 'Socrates says.' You banged the
table as if it were Socrates and said, 'Curse
Socrates'." That I know to be true, though I am
also sure that it is of a later date than where my
old narrative puts it, which is in the first year
of our marriage, before Monty was born (I actually
undermine the trustworthiness of my own account by
recalling how "the children were asleep", so more
than one, and meaning that it must have been much
later!) It would also have been unlikely that I
would have known Nietzsche unless Else had sent me
something.

In 1900, I was pregnant, too; and I was sick for
a couple of months. I did so much want Ernst to
love me – he was all I had – and I felt that I was
probably disgusting to him.

But perhaps even worse was that at first I saw no
way I could ever fit into everyday English life.
I learned the form of it from Ernst's cook and
maid Laura, who continued to come in (she only
went home at night). On Monday the cold joint
from Sunday (when he was at home, Ernst always
proudly carved the Sunday joint), and then Tuesday

washday. How long the washing took to dry in the
damp Nottingham air! The ironing was done on
Wednesday and cleaning carried out on Thursday and
Friday. And kitchen cleaning on Saturday. I was
"at home" on Thursday afternoons and sang in a
choir on Fridays. And Ernst's friends the
Kippings, him a colleague, were always so helpful
and thoughtful, always ready to advise me on the
habits and prejudices of English life.

  Yet I also knew that I did not fit in. Only when
my mother came over, for the birth of Monty in my
first summer in Nottingham, did I feel I could
actually communicate what I felt; and I had to be
careful with her, too, so as not to be disloyal to
Ernst and all he was trying to do for me.

  But even after the birth of my other two
children, I never really lost the feeling that I
was living on the surface of life in Nottingham.
After my first fascinated attraction to Ernst my
feelings grew weaker and weaker. He never gave me
any joy. And nothing or almost nothing went deep:
only my games with the children, as they grew up,
and the wonderful sense of happiness they brought
me, made me feel at one with myself. Ernst made
love to me every night almost without fail, except
before and after the birth of the children, but it
only ever felt like a sometimes mildly enjoyable
marital duty (on my part) and a marital right (on
his) mixed up with a strange kind of adoration of
my person which also involved his making love to
me as violently as possible, almost as if he were
trying to destroy me, to knock me off the pedestal
he had put me on. Well, perhaps not that exactly,
but it felt something like that. He wanted me to
sit on him sometimes, which was at least a change,
though it did not excite me at all; then he wanted
to make love to me in my other possibility, too (I
don't know how to put this nicely, I don't like
the word "bugger"), but I would not allow that and
literally fought back with my nails when he tried
it. Did that ever happen to you, Betsy? No, you
don't have to answer!

After the birth of Barby in what I think must have been 1904 (we celebrated her fiftieth last year, how astonishing), we moved house and Ernst was also away almost the whole summer in Cambridge, lecturing. This gave me the chance to have my own room and my own bed and I really, really enjoyed it. I had always found our Dr Stafford very menschlich and sympathisch and I was seeing him, anyway, after the birth, and I mentioned how agreeable it was to be on my own more, and he asked me if I would like him to put the idea to Ernst that I should have no more children? I thought that was a wonderful idea, and I nodded and cheerfully said "Ja!" It was not actually that I did not want any more children, but that I would like to escape from at least some of what Ernst called his "attentions" (they never attended to me much, those "attentions" of his).

And so while Ernst was away I had the house and its rooms reorganized so that I had my own room – with my bed in it – and he had his own dressing room (something he had always wanted) though that meant he was no longer next to my room; so we gave him his own sleeping room too, next to his dressing room.

And Dr Stafford must have said something to him, I don't exactly know what, but it must have been about my not having any more children, because he started only coming to me when I had Tante Rosa visiting (I had always warned him about her visits, when I was peculiarly listless and bad-tempered), and not always then. I confess I never missed him; and when he did come into my bed, I liked it even less than before, but I felt I should not deprive him of myself entirely, I am not sure why: an old feeling about rights, I suppose, meaning the fact that I <u>had</u> married him.

It was during the year after Barby was born that I
had my first lover. Somehow Ernst knew this
couple the Dowsons, in their early fifties; he a
business-man, but really unconventional, with one
of the first cars in Nottinghamshire, she a worker
for the women's suffrage. They were not the kinds
of people Ernst usually saw or made friends with,
but I got to know them when my children were still
very young, and Ernst suggested that Dowson would
be an excellent godfather for the new one, Barby,
as he would certainly look after her financially.
Following that I saw more of them. She was sad, I
thought, though also heroic in the kinds of thing
she had set out to do!

He became a friend of ours, though we did not see
him very often; he was older than Ernst but mostly
felt younger. One Sunday night when we were at
their house, he offered to take us out in his
brand new car the next day (the weather was good,
and it promised to be a warm day: this was the
spring of 1905). I asked Ernst (who was always
busy on Mondays) if I might go and he said that I
could go if I would be certain not to catch cold
and then give it to him. So we set off, with me
dressed up in hats and scarves, as was the fashion
in those days, and Dowson - I never called him
William, I don't think I called him anything —
drove me to Sherwood Forest, to a part where I had
never been. I was so impressed with how the great
hoary oaks stood, far apart from each other.
There were also pools of bluebells between them,
and I remember that the primroses were as big as
pennies.

The trip had been a great success, and he
promised to take me again when he had another free
day . . . and a month or so later, when it was
really warm, he dropped a note to me and to Ernst
asking if we would both like to come. Again Ernst
couldn't; again I asked if I might, and Ernst was
happy once again. This time we went to another
part of the Forest, one less well-known, Dowson

said; and with the hood of the car down, we sat in the shade and talked. I asked him about his wife and he told me a lot about them and their marriage. He also told an awful story about how he had once proposed to her, when they were both still young, that she should take off her clothes one moonlit night, and make love with him under the moon: and she had refused, not just once but over and over. And following that she had also told him that she found a man's body ugly, "all in parts, with mechanical joints". After that they had hardly slept together anymore; and that had been years ago. I told him that I would have taken my clothes off in broad daylight, not just in moonlight; and he said he would have chased me through the wood to make sure I did. And that is exactly what we ended up doing, running through the trees like mad things, with me throwing my hat and my coat away as I ran; and he caught me, and we made love.

When I accepted him, at least I felt that he appreciated me a bit; but our love-making was always so rushed that we had no time to enjoy it. At least, I didn't. This first time, out in the woods, was in some ways the best of all; he was a very busy man, and though he only lived around the corner in Nottingham, we could never see each other much. I think he was mostly pleased with himself for having conquered me, and that was a feeling I did not like at all. And it was all so infrequent; three or four times altogether over two years at most, I think.

He made me feel, for a little while, desirable, and that was good. But he also had no idea how to bring me satisfaction, or more likely no interest in doing so, and I confess that when I was considering how to tell my sexual life story of these years, I almost forgot to include him. Our affair simply didn't go anywhere or lead to anything. It was just a passing excitement. Life was actually easier without him, as it turned out. (When I told Lawrence about what had happened, he

could do very little with it in his writing,
either, which was unusual, as he used almost
everything I ever told him about my young life,
especially my sexual experiences. It was only
very late, when he wrote Lady C, that he used it a
bit.)

8

During this time, however, Else had been writing
to me about the young analyst Otto Gross, who had
married our old friend Friedele Schloffer; and in
the end it became clear to me, simply from her
letters, that Otto had become Else's lover too.
In fact, early in 1907 she became pregnant by him.
She had told me that he was a marvelous lover,
which intrigued me, as I knew that Else was not
given to compliments of that kind (she had for
example told me that she found the attentions of
her husband Alfred mostly a nuisance and never
enjoyable at all). So when I went to Muenchen in
the spring of 1907 I looked forward to meeting
this Otto.

He turned out to be even younger than I had
imagined; he came from the Austrian Alps and had
the light strong frame of a mountaineer; he was
also the first vegetarian I had ever met. "I
won't eat your nasty carcasses", he would say, and
he drank no alcohol.

It would be wrong to say he threw himself at me.
That was not at all how he was. He just took it
for granted that we would soon be going to bed
together. The following day I found myself going
round to his flat in the Tuerkenstrasse (he and
his wife only sometimes lived together) and found
him overpoweringly attractive. In a kind of
trance there I was taking my clothes off and
getting into bed with him, and he was
unhesitatingly making love to me.

And I was amazed. He talked all the time. He
went out of his way to talk to me as we had sex
and he told me over and over how wonderful it was
and how I was the finest woman he had ever had.
And at the time I certainly believed it. And he
wanted to arouse me and he did; he knew how, by
staying in me after his orgasm and letting me
move. He stayed hard, I don't know how he did it,
and soon I came and came. And after Otto, I never
wanted a lover who wouldn't treat me as he had
treated me, and who would not be able to arouse me

as he had done, and who did not want me to have my
orgasms too. I think I actually had my first
orgasm with Otto, certainly the first one which I
knew was an orgasm, and which he enjoyed too, and
told me about, which I also found most arousing.
But most of all he caressed me all over, touched
me and entered me with his fingers and caused me
to quiver all over with the sensations he was
giving me. Being in bed with him was quite
extraordinary; those afternoons were among the
best of my life.

I did not know whether to tell Else what was
happening, but I was sure that she would find out
soon, from Otto, who never had any sense of
discretion or of other people's feelings, or she
might hear possibly from Friedele. So I left it
to them to tell her. Sadly, in real desperation,
because I had fallen deeply in love with him – at
last I knew what that meant! – I had rather soon
to go back to England, but very soon afterwards I
got Edgar to write inviting me to Holland, where
he and Else were going to be, together with Otto,
at a conference. So I went back, and met Otto
again; and this time he traveled with me on the
night boat back from Holland to England, and we
made love, and it was if possible even more
wonderful than before. When he begged me to stay
with him for good, I found it almost impossible to
refuse. We did together the most impossible
things, such as making love on deck on the boat,
under the stars. He was such a marvelous lover.
I was desperately in love with him (I remember
writing to him that loving him was as necessary to
me as breathing) and I was also deeply in love
with his vision of a new society. He saw the
world as a large growing place with endless
possibilities, and I believed him and knew that it
could all change and that I could change too; so
much I wanted fun and adventure and mystery, but
also a better state for women like me. I actually
felt myself to be what he kept insisting I was,
the woman of the future. The only question was:

how to get this future to come. Even my children knew that something important had happened. Barby was quite uncanny; when I got back from Holland, she said to me "You are not our old mother. You have got our old mother's skin on, but you are not our mother that went away." I lived for Otto's letters, which came regularly via Else or Edgar, and were long and exciting, so that I felt utterly torn between my life in Nottingham and the life he was inviting me to share, as the new and regenerated person I felt myself to be. Nottingham was unbearable, the people utterly dull and lifeless, Ernst a hopeless person to whom I felt I was shackled.

But I also loved my children; they fascinated me, their difference of character, the things they said and did, and the fun I always had with them (on Sunday mornings they all came into my bedroom and my bed, and we had pillow-fights). When Monty went to school, I would stand at the window making faces at him, and though he liked it he would also look up a little anxious that nobody else could see me. I seemed so much nearer to my children than to the grown-up people, with the exception of Otto.

But here was Otto, so utterly attuned to me, and (I believed) deeply in love with me. It was only with great difficulty that I told myself that this was exactly what Else must be feeling, and Friedele too, and goodness how many other women, and that he did not find me special, only new; and that probably all of us were to him women of the future, not just me. I told myself this; and in the end Else told me the same. But I also did not believe it.

I used to think Otto the most important person in my young life. I don't any more. He said some marvelous and extremely influential things to me, as when he told me that he thought I was the only living human being who "has remained free" from all the accumulated rubbish of society, remained free "through your own strength"; when he told me

I was "born for freedom", when he called me a "genius" who permitted him actually to see his "dream of a future" (you see, I can still quote these things: I still keep his letters!) And I loved him so desperately.

Not for a moment did I really believe that I was as wonderful as Otto said, but at the time I was thrilled by his vision of a better world, one that was happier and better than the normal world, and more charitable, because free.

When I look back now, however, I fear that all he really did was produce wonderful theoretical phrases, in his letters and in what he said to me. He made me a type of woman; he never thought about me as a living individual (it just strikes me that he was like Ernst in this, though not in any other way!) He told me I was a woman who gave him the hope of a marvelous future, but he was incapable of giving me any actual future, one lived with him, which was what I so much wanted. He insisted that there was an unbreakable bond between us, but there was also something sadly wrong in him, as I slowly realized. Else said that he totally lacked self-control, which was probably true, but even worse to me was the fact that he did not have his feet on the ground of reality. He ignored or rejected my argument that I could not, for example, just abandon my marriage, simply walk away from a good husband like Ernst, or from my children. And the thought of my children and their needs was luckily enough to hold me back from ever committing myself to him, though I admit I was deeply tempted, and felt tortured by his flattery and his invitations, and in the end by the fact of losing him and his love. But the children always served to remind me of the reality which mattered. Else also wrote to me, when I was deep in despair about him, that a life together with Otto and three children was "absolutely unthinkable", that is what she said. She also said she thought Ernst's love for me was much greater than Otto's, which was probably true,

though it was not at all what I wanted to hear at
the time!

At any rate, eventually I decided to stay with my
children, to begin with simply by telling myself
that somehow I could at least keep them, and still
go on having Otto love me, seeing him at least
occasionally, and that this way of living could
continue perhaps for years. I was wrong. Otto
became disillusioned with me; he probably felt I
was giving him up, which was true in a way, though
I also now feel fairly sure that he had found some
other woman to tell all the things he had been
telling me: that she was the woman of the future,
and so on. I shall never know. Anyway, I went on
feeling that my life had changed utterly, but I
was quite unable to demonstrate how, except in the
feelings which no-one saw. Feeling that sex
should be free, I even tried sleeping with Ernst
again, but after Otto it was no good, and I
stopped after a week or so (I forget what excuse I
gave). It was, however, around now that I started
to dance by myself; on Sunday mornings I would
take most of my clothes off and dance around in my
room and think spitefully and happily of all the
stupid people in Nottingham going to church. That
helped a bit, at least at the time.

But though I was now prepared for experiences
outside my marriage, and actually looked forward
to them, nothing much happened over the next four
years. This was perhaps just as well, because
Ernst was suddenly very ill in, I think, 1910, and
for months I had to act as nurse, which was new to
me, and I do not think I was very good at it! I
learned a good deal more about how to behave with
a sick person, sadly, when with Lawrence. This
illness of Ernst kept me at home for the whole of
the spring and summer, and I could not pay my
usual annual visit with one or two of the children
to Germany.

However, then, one of the men Else had met in
Ascona, when there with Otto, had been a painter
named Ernst Frick; and when I finally managed to
go and see Else, in 1911, it turned out that Frick

too was in Muenchen; he was very close to Otto's
wife Friedele (eventually, I believe, they even
had a number of children together).

He was an extraordinary man. Born in
Switzerland, he was an anarchist, and also a
wonderful artist, with a face which reminded me of
the side of an axe, with a marvelous great nose.
He was either extraordinarily beautiful, or
extraordinarily ugly, depending on whether one
liked him. I liked him very much indeed, and
found him wonderful looking; and in 1911 he
actually traveled back to England with me, when I
returned from my annual visit to the Continent.
He had lodgings in London (he had political
friends there, I think) but he also came to
Nottingham; and I saw him too in London, where he
had started painting.

He had however no interest in marriage or in
settled relationships, or in my children, as he
made perfectly clear to me; he was very honest,
just an excellent lover, if never often enough in
my bed (we managed it in Nottingham just once,
when Ernst was away in Cambridge, and I had to
tell fibs to the children about why this
extraordinary foreign man was in the house on a
Sunday morning). In the autumn of 1911, however,
he had to go back to Muenchen, and we kept in
touch by letter; but he was not a good letter
writer. I saw him again in 1913 though by then he
was living with Friedele. But I thought then that
he and Lawrence could do something together; he
could have designed the setting for one of
Lawrence's plays, for example.

But apart from those few times with Frick, I
simply got older, and had come to think myself as
simply not lovable, with three children and a
settled life in Nottingham. But although I went
on behaving perfectly normally, bright and
cheerful as ever, as I had been told to be and
encouraged to be, all my life, and had also
developed friendships with the daughters of our
old neighbors the Bradleys, Madge and Gladys, to

whom I explained some of Otto's beliefs about
women and the future, I was also really miserable
inside. I could see no way forward, only the
depressing, temporary pleasures of social life,
and could hope only for my children, especially
for Monty and Barbara. I never felt quite the
same about Elsa, I do not know why; she had
somehow become Ernst's child, not mine. That
happens. And of course she looked after him in
his old age.

10

Lawrence was a young and not much published writer
when I first met him in the spring of 1912, and he
struck me at once as a man who although clearly
attracted to me was far too young for me (he was
actually six years younger). He could talk all
right, and could indeed be fascinating, but in his
own way he seemed as impossible as a future
partner as Otto would have been, simply because he
was so inexperienced in the ways of the world, in
fact hardly belonged to the world of work at all
(he had given up his job, and was relying upon the
little he had saved, and the next payment from his
publisher). He had never had children and had had
such bad experiences with women that he actually
said he wanted nothing more to do with them; and
that felt adolescent to me, as well as off-
putting!

He had no money, being the son of a coalminer and
now an unemployed teacher, and I knew that for a
future with my children I had to have a decent
income: while even an affair, in my experience,
was at times expensive, as it meant travel and
sometimes hotels. In spite of his attraction to
me, and the things he wrote to me, calling me
wonderful, I felt I could rule him out except as a
young man who would be nice to me when I felt
miserable. And because Ernst said that there was
nothing he could do for him (Lawrence was planning
a trip to Germany, which was why he had originally
come to see us), I obviously would not be seeing
much more of him.

In Not I, But the Wind! in 1933 I wrote a version
of our first meeting which is very far from the
truth, now I look back at it. I thought that I
had to do a necessary job "advertising" Lawrence.
Now I do not feel that need, he is so famous, and
I can tell the truth, which is that our way
towards finding each other as partners was full of
problems! I was trying to "sell" Lawrence in the
1930s, I needed an income and for him to have a
good reputation. So in my exciting version of our

meeting I described how we were attracted to each other from the first. I wanted to present him as someone who knew what he wanted and who had found in me a person who also knew what she wanted. (Betsy, just type out the paragraphs I have marked in my copy, pages 22 to 23).

*   *   *

"I see him before me as he entered the house. A long thin figure, quick straight legs, light, sure movements. He seemed so obviously simple. Yet he arrested my attention. There was something more than met the eye. What kind of a bird was this?

The half-hour before lunch the two of us talked in my room, French windows open, curtains fluttering in the spring wind, my children playing on the lawn.

He said he had finished with his attempts at knowing women. I was amazed at the way he fiercely denounced them. I had never before heard anything like it. I laughed, yet I could tell he had tried very hard, and had cared. We talked about Oedipus and understanding leaped through our words.

After leaving, that night, he walked all the way to his home. It was a walk of at least five hours. Soon afterwards he wrote to me: You are the most wonderful woman in all England.

I wrote back: You don't know many women in England, how do you know? He also told me, the second time we met, 'You are quite unaware of your husband, you take no notice of him.' I really disliked the directness of this criticism (though I now recognize how perceptive and accurate it was).

He came on Easter Sunday. It was a bright, sunny day. The children were in the garden hunting for Easter eggs."

*   *   *

I should explain that this Easter Sunday was when Ernst was away meeting other academics for a conference in Cambridge; that was why I was alone with the children and without even Ida and Bertha, who had a holiday. But it was also most embarrassing, as I go on to explain.

*   *   *

"The maids were out and I wanted to make some tea.
I tried to turn on the gas but didn't know how.
Lawrence became cross at such ignorance. Such a
direct critic! He never hid such things behind
politeness, though he could be very polite when he
chose. But such criticism was something my High
and Mightiness was very little accustomed to.

Yet Lawrence really understood me. From the
first he saw through me like glass, saw how hard I
was trying to keep up a cheerful front. I thought
it was so despicable and unproud and unclean to be
miserable, but he saw through my hard bright
shell.

What I cannot understand is how he could have
loved me and wanted me at that time. I certainly
did have what he called sex in the head: a theory
of loving men. My real self was frightened and
shrank from contact like a wild thing.

So our relationship developed."

*   *   *

But, no, it did not develop. He wanted to see me,
and tried to see me, but we cannot have been
together more than four or five times in all, and
only had sex once, out in Clifton, which was
exciting but not good at all; that was almost the
only time we were alone together, without the
children. We managed to go to the theatre
together once, and saw a play by Shaw, when Madge
Bradley gave me her ticket and I could give it to
Lawrence. But on that visit on Easter Sunday we
had the children, as we did on a trip I made out
one afternoon into the country. I wrote about
that:

*   *   *

"One day we met at a station in Derbyshire. My two
small girls were with us. We went for a long walk
through the early-spring woods and fields. The
children were running here and there as young
creatures will.

We came to a small brook, a little stone bridge

crossed it. Lawrence made the children some paper
boats and put matches in them and let them float
downstream under the bridge. Then he put daisies
in the brook, and they floated down with their
upturned faces. Crouched by the brook, playing
there with the children, Lawrence forgot about me
completely.

Suddenly I knew I loved him. He had touched a
new tenderness in me. After that, things happened
quickly."

*   *   *

That is not actually the case. Things did not
happen quickly. Even managing to get on the same
train to Germany was full of difficulties. And
Lawrence's letters to me all had to go via the
Bradleys, and I could not always collect them when
I wanted. Other things were also difficult and
different from what I wrote: what my children
thought, for example. Barby later told me, before
Not I was published in fact, that they had not
taken to Lawrence at all, on those meetings out in
the country; they much preferred the academic
kinds of men they had met in Nottingham, who were
cheerful and nice. My old narrative goes on:

*   *   *

"He came to see me one Sunday. My husband was away
and I said: Stay the night with me. 'No, I will
not stay in your husband's house while he is away,
but you must tell him the truth and we will go
away together, because I love you.'

I was frightened. I knew how terrible such a
thing would be for my husband, he had always
trusted me. But a force stronger than myself made
me deal him the blow. I left the next day. I left
my son with his father, my two little girls I took
to their grandparents in London. I said good-bye
to them on Hampstead Heath, blind and blank with
pain, dimly feeling I should never again live with
them as I had done.

Lawrence met me at Charing Cross Station, to go
away with him, never to leave him again.

He seemed to have lifted me body and soul out of

45

all my past life. This young man of twenty-six had
taken all my fate, all my destiny, into his hands.
And we had known each other barely for six weeks.
There had been nothing else for me to do but
submit."

*   *   *

I wrote all that more then twenty years ago, and
don't know today how I did it! Bits of it seem
all right, but most of it now feels like romance,
not at all like the truth. When for example I say
"I left the next day", I make myself sound so sure
and determined. But it was not a bit like that.
Even the day I was leaving was not decided until
the last minute. I did not tell Ernst that I was
in love with another man, either, although I had
meant to, and it was partly true: and I had no
idea I was losing my daughters. Above all
Lawrence was not the compelling "force stronger
than myself" which this account makes him: and I
certainly never "submitted" to him. I never left
for a future with him at all. We had had sex
again, quickly and not very well, a few days
before we left, nothing else.

For one thing, although he had insisted to me
that I must tell Ernst about our affair (we had
been in London together, and had then visited his
friend Garnett's place in Kent), and I had
promised to do so, I simply didn't. Instead I
told Ernst about Dowson and Gross, as they were in
the past, and I thought it be easier for Ernst to
start there. I had agreed to talk to him to try
and make my going away more honest, but in fact it
didn't at all; I ended up swearing that I was no
longer having an affair with either of them, but
Ernst did not believe me; and by then it was far
too late to talk about Lawrence too. So it was
all just a terrible mess.

I am also quite sure that I did not wonder,
before leaving, if I would ever again live with my
children as I had done. I had no such thoughts at
all. My worries about the children all came
later. I wrote that to make my subsequent actions

look better, to show that I was worried and concerned about them from the start.

I think that I really had no care for such things, in all the haste and trouble of leaving. What I had really been hoping for was just the pleasure of having a new man waiting for me at the railway station, thoroughly in love with me and ready to take me away with him. But now I had to worry about Ernst's anger too.

I had, too, not the least idea that this was a journey which would see me ending my marriage. Lawrence had certainly not lifted me out of my past life; so far as I was concerned, my old life was certainly going to go on just as it had been, with – I hoped – the occasional nice young man in it, to make me feel better, and probably just the occasional rage in Ernst.

In Not I, over and over again I made everything sound so much easier than it actually was, and Lawrence so much more determined and me so much more certain and responsive. I wrote like that to make myself sound better, and also Lawrence!

I should also have said around here that on one occasion before we left, Ernst met Lawrence late at night, at Private Road, and almost threw him out of the house before shouting at me for being stupid, in allowing myself to be pursued at all hours by such an unacceptable man; but that did not seem to matter much to me.

One real trouble was that, in Not I, I did not want to write about Ernst. I did not even name him, and I could not really explain what was wrong with my way of life in Nottingham that I wanted so badly to leave it; and I also did not want to mention my other affairs, in case they detracted from the importance of my relationship with Lawrence. Now I can do all those things.

But I want now to describe what happened when I
came to Metz with Lawrence as my lover, I imagined
just for this single visit, in May 1912. The
reason for my trip, so early in the year, was the
celebration of my father's fifty years in the
army, which Ernst certainly did not want to
attend, but which the children also would not have
enjoyed, so I had left them behind for once.
It was, strangely, considering how tenderly he
felt for me, Lawrence who did the real damage to
my relationship with Ernst and cost me my
children. We had gone to Metz together, by train,
hoping for this week together before he was due to
go up to the Rheinland to his relations; and after
Metz I had planned to go to my sister in Bavaria
for a week or so as well. That was all worked
out. It felt in fact like a very nice kind of
running away together, quite safe because I was a
bit sadly certain that after Bavaria I would be
going back to Ernst and the children; and Lawrence
too assumed that I would be going back. But I
liked Lawrence very much indeed, even though he
was not yet at all a good lover. As a person,
though, I knew that he responded always to the
person I was, not to the person he wanted me to
be; he saw deeply into me. And we had the chance
of this week together.
From the train I had taken him to his protestant
lodging house, a big dull brown place, der
Deutscher Hof, in a narrow little street just down
from the Cathedral, and arranged where to see him
later that afternoon . . . then I had to go down
to Montigny, to all my family. Later that same
afternoon I came back into town with my mother; we
went to have tea together in the Wilhelmsgarten,
as we always did, and Lawrence joined us there,
meeting us as if by chance. My mother looked
sharply at him but did not wish to ask more; she
used her remnants of English, and he struggled
with German phrases. Luckily the cake took a lot
of eating, so that there were few conversational

pauses. I had to behave towards him as a person
from Nottingham whom I knew only a little and who
I was surprised to meet in Metz. He had to take
on the personality of a business-man, like Dowson,
who was here to do business. I told him that if
he wished to meet my sister Else, who spoke such
good English, then he should come to the Cathedral
tomorrow at two, while my mother politely invited
him for lunch at our home on Tuesday. And then
she and I left together, though I could see how
disappointed Lawrence was, having hoped to get me
to his hotel: was that not why we had come to Metz
together?

  But it was actually a relief for a moment to be
away from these men's demands – Lawrence's but
also Ernst's – at home in Montigny with all my
family for the celebrations, even though home was
bursting with people (my uncle from Berlin was
there, for example); there were so many of us that
I had to share a room, with Else. But at least to
be away from Nottingham was wonderful. I wondered
if Else would see from my manner what had happened
to me, and that I had a new lover, but she did not
seem to: she was so busy telling me about her
feelings for Max and for Alfred. Nothing was
planned for that Saturday evening; the first
celebration for my father was going to be a family
dinner on Sunday night. But, as we went for a
walk, I told Else that there was an Englishman in
town whom I would like her to meet. She smiled
ironically and said that she hoped I was being
discreet and careful. But I also wanted to get to
bed, being exhausted from the night on the train.

  Everything changed on the Sunday morning. A
letter had actually come for me the previous day,
but with all these people arriving it had been
forgotten, and I only got it at breakfast on the
Sunday. It was from Ernst, and quite short. As I
remember it, it ended up saying something like "I
think you have recently had a lover. If that is
true, wire me GANZ RECENT". I did not at all
expect this and did not know what to do. I would

be returning to Nottingham after my weeks away, my return ticket was in my valise, but I could clearly not wait for long before answering such a letter. I found Else, who had gone back to our room after breakfast to read, and told her I had to talk to her. And I told her the whole story, and asked her what I should wire.

Her advice was very simple. She spoke to me as she had always done: understandingly, but also firmly. She said that although I had this new lover, I must not allow my marriage to be endangered in such a stupid way. I must wire back "Untrue: am here alone", which was certainly what Ernst wanted to hear. And then, in a month's time, when I was back in Nottingham, she suggested that I could start to explain that I needed to spend more time on my own; that naturally I wanted my marriage to continue, but that I needed a new basis for it. She was as sure as she had been when I was in love with Otto that, if I now tried to tell Ernst the truth, he would not listen but would end my marriage and take my children away.

I explained that there was no chance that a man like Ernst would accept any other basis for our marriage than the one we had. But Else insisted that she knew men through and through, and there was nothing they would not do if they believed they could also go on making love to you. If you threatened them with having no longer access to you in bed, you could bargain your way into almost anything. I did not tell her that, following what the doctor had said to Ernst, I hardly ever slept with Ernst any more. Nor did I tell her that, under pressure from Lawrence, I had already told Weekley about Dowson and Gross, and that had started the trouble and made him suspicious.

Anyway, at two o'clock we went to the cathedral, and Lawrence again immediately saw us. Else had much better English than our mother, and was able to talk with him pretty easily. We went into the Wilhelmsgarten to have coffee there and I recall that Lawrence again did not offer to pay anything,

which I thought a bit mean, it was the second time
in two days that my family had provided him with
coffee and cake. We sat on chairs in the shade,
under the lilacs, and I produced Ernst's letter
and read it aloud, and Else translated the hard
bits for Lawrence.

But he was, in his own and very different way,
just as certain as Else: he exploded, and insisted
that I must wire "GANZ RECENT", exactly as Ernst
demanded, as that was the truth. And he also
insisted that I write to Ernst, too, explaining
that I was here with him. He offered to write to
Ernst as well, if I thought that a good idea.

Else listened, as she always did, but then spoke
very firmly to say that Lawrence was quite wrong,
that I must continue to be married if I was to
keep my children and maintain any freedom for the
future; and that, after these few days in Metz,
Lawrence must simply wait until I could get away
again (I had explained that he was on his way to
the Rheinland). Else was sure that something
could be managed, back in Nottingham. She said
that she knew Ernst and that it was no good
telling him the truth, he would react so horribly
and hysterically.

Then she went off and Lawrence and I went down to
his hotel and I got in without the manageress
seeing me, and we went up to his room, right up
under the rafters, and took our clothes off and at
last he made love to me in the big bed he had.
That, however, was also all in a hurry and really
not good, as we were both thinking of other
things. But he said again that he could not live
without me and that we must talk about our future:
"let's go away from Metz", he kept saying. But I
did not feel free and was not at all sure about
"our" future; I was still a married woman and
loved my children.

I had to get back home as I was expected to
dinner but I promised to come back to him early
the next morning. That evening I told Nusch about
Lawrence and Ernst, to find that she absolutely

agreed with Else. Both my sisters had already reached what I might call accommodations with husbands whom they no longer loved, but they had stayed married. And the important thing was that they could do pretty much what they wanted, and their husbands supported them, and they had their children.

They thought Lawrence was hopelessly wrong for me: not wrong as Otto had been wrong, because Lawrence was (Else had seen) an extremely charming and clever person, but wrong because he had no money, and had no job, and because he was obviously incapable of providing a home for me and the children. I was terribly conscious of how everything and everybody was against my coming together with Lawrence, and I agreed that, in almost every way, it seemed crazy. And I remained very much in two minds about it; I still thought it was just a holiday romance, however nice it was.

Against that, Lawrence was so certain that we had to stay together, but Else was equally certain, and also – I knew – far more sensible. I did not go to his hotel on the Monday morning after all. It was anyway difficult with all the preparations and dressing up for my father's big day: but I did not want to go either. During the Monday I hardly saw him either, as I had to be with my family for the celebrations. There was just a moment when we glimpsed each other, in the fair in the town, but I could not acknowledge him as I was walking with my father. Nusch though had a few words with him after Else pointed him out, discreetly, and afterwards she told me what a nice man she thought he was.

I got a letter from him, though, which he had brought round to our house, telling me that he would be back in his hotel at 2.30 in the afternoon; but it was quite impossible for me to go then either. He also suggested that I count on my fingers our remaining days in Germany, and then compare them with the days in Nottingham that would follow – and be shocked. And he declared it was the last day when he would not insist on seeing me. But that was how it had to be.

Only on the Tuesday morning could I see him again properly. When we met, at the cathedral again, he began at once complaining that we were seeing even less of each other than we had done in Nottingham! (which was true). What he most wanted to know, though, was what I had wired to Ernst, and what I had said in my letter to him. I told him I had not yet sent either a wire or a letter and he looked very concerned.

We had wanted to go for a walk together out of town, so as to meet no-one we knew, but unluckily we passed by a telegraph office and he was more than ever insistent that I must at least wire to Ernst, and I knew I certainly had to soon . . . and he wanted me to set things straight, once and for all. After all, he insisted that we loved each other and we could face anything, put up with anything, together. He walked in with me; and there, with him standing beside me, insisting so wonderfully that he could make a life for me better than any I had known before, which I very much wanted to believe, and that he loved me so much, I did what he was asking me to do, though I knew a bit how dangerous it was. I wired "GANZ RECENT".

It was certainly the admission of a recent lover but not in itself, I thought, the end of my marriage, and I was not at all sure how Ernst would react. I admit that I had the wicked thought that he might behave like his elder brother, and do away with himself on getting the news that I no longer loved him, so leaving me free. What I did not expect was that my telegram would end so much: I was still full of hope for the future, though what kind of a future it would be I did not know.

We then wandered down a lane, and I was so
concerned about what I had just done, and what
might follow from it, that I did not notice where
we were going, or what this nice grassy bank was,
where we sat down and then lay down. Lawrence
urgently wanted to make love to me but it was too
public. But all the same he had his hand up under
my dress and was caressing me intimately (these
were the days before knickers, Betsy, but I am
sorry, I am making you blush) when we heard this
voice behind us telling us to stand up as we were
being arrested for trespassing.

It was only a boy soldier and very quickly I
quietened him down by telling him that my father
was Baron Friedrich von Richthofen, who was just
celebrating fifty years in the army! But all the
same he insisted on taking our names, and he got
terribly interested when he found out that
Lawrence was English. He had heard us talking in
a foreign language and now he told us he would
have to report us for entering an enclosed
military area, and that Lawrence was under
suspicion of spying, and he insisted on having
Lawrence's address in England and in Germany too.

Lawrence was rather upset, he had never
encountered so many soldiers as he had in Metz and
he had said how much he disliked them. Now he was
in their hands, so to speak; and he insisted that
I inform the soldier that he couldn't tell the
difference between a fortress and a factory.

I thought however that this little episode hardly
mattered as this was the day when we were due to
have lunch with my family in Montigny, and I could
give my father a version of what had happened, and
Lawrence could explain who he was (using the
personality he had developed the previous time),
and that would be that; and we were already late,
so we had to hurry back.

My father looked worried for a moment when I told
him about the young soldier but then he laughed.
He and Lawrence got on very badly, however; they

had to talk in French, and I could hear him correcting Lawrence's errors in grammar, which Lawrence would have hated. And Lawrence had to tell so many fibs about why he was in Metz at all and how he knew me; it was not really very convincing, and everything felt wrong. After lunch was over I explained that I needed to take Lawrence out to show him where the tram was which would take back to his hotel, but Lawrence was furious over what had happened, first with the young soldier and then with my father, and also over how he had had to tell all those lies. We agreed that I would come to his hotel early the following morning, or if that proved impossible I would come at midday. And he insisted again that I must write that letter to Ernst, and that he would not be happy until I did.

It was when he got back to his hotel, however, that he must have written quite a long note repeating how he could not stand telling any more lies, and enclosing an example of the letter which he wanted me to send to Ernst. And he brought these down to Montigny and put them in the letter-box (I got them later that afternoon). He also said that he would hang on in Metz until Ernst sent an "answer to the truth".

So I had tc write to Ernst and tell "the truth"! I liked Lawrence's letter to him but knew that it went far too far; that it would mean the end of my marriage, for certain. I could not send it.

My father, however, had rained questions down on me when I got back to the family; he had demanded to know whether Lawrence were my lover, and when I refused to answer he declared that I was behaving disgracefully, that no daughter of his, etc. etc. But, much worse, late that afternoon when I was out with my mother, without telling me he got Else to go to Lawrence's hotel and pass on the message that the military authorities were not happy with his presence in the town, that they suspected that he was an English officer, and that they advised him to leave immediately, before they had to act officially, when he would certainly be arrested. Whether this was true or not, I never knew; it is possible that my father just invented it, but when I got back and heard about it I believed it as well.

Else had, of course, been extremely happy to go and tell Lawrence the news, and to give him the advice that he should go to Trier, eighty miles away, first thing next morning. And Lawrence also naturally believed everything she said. He had almost no money, but luckily Nusch had brought money with her, and Else could lend him a hundred Marks. And she told him she was sure I would manage to come to the station.

I was very angry when I found out what had happened, and blamed my father for not getting the spying thing cleared up, which I was sure he could have done. But even worse was the fact that Ernst that same evening sent me a telegram in return for mine: "KEINE MOEGLICHKEIT" – "no possibility". Everything was piling up and I found it very difficult to know what to do. I told Else about it and together we wrote a letter to Ernst at once, insisting that he and I must find a compromise; and I also arranged to go to the station the following morning to tell Lawrence how awkward the situation had become.

When I got there, I found that Lawrence was not as upset as I thought he would be at having to go away; the reason being that he had written out and posted his letter to Weekley about his love for me, a letter he said was very similar to the one he had sent to me. I thought at the time that it was a brave but also a terribly foolish thing to have done, much worse than the telegram, and events showed that it was.

But he really wanted me, and as he believed he needed to leave Metz, he wanted to do something to stop me going back to Ernst, something which he was still very frightened my family might persuade me to do. All I could do was refuse his demand that I should come down to Trier at once, and I managed to put it off to the Saturday, by which time things should at least have quietened down a bit.

Following this episode with Lawrence, however, I got on terribly badly with both my parents. My father was insistent that I had taken the very worst kind of man as a lover, Lawrence being (in his words) "a clumsy clown" who had no right trying to seduce a woman like me. My mother, whom I took more seriously, was voluble about the way I was wrecking my marriage for nothing; she was also terribly anxious about my children. And I was angry with my father for not getting the spying charge dropped.

And then, on the Friday, to make things still worse, my father got a letter from Ernst telling him that all was over between him and me and that he was moving the children to London. This was awful. My parents were in a rage with what they called my stupidity and insisted that I write and wire to Ernst to try and stop him. I wired to him offering to come and help by bringing the girls back from London. The only things this week not so terrible were the letters which Lawrence was writing to me from Trier: "Bis Samstag", he had written, "till Saturday", and he added "ich liebe dich schwer" (by which he probably meant "I love you terribly"). It was as well that he did, because I was all too conscious that for me this was not a grand passion, that I had only expected a lover for a week or so, not a man prepared to fight my husband for me. I was not at all sure that I wanted Lawrence to fight Ernst, or even wanted him as a permanent partner, and I certainly did not want to marry him. Above all I wished to safeguard my children.

On the Friday night I announced that I was going to Trier to see him but my father absolutely forbade it. Confrontation across the dinner table! Only when my mother offered to come with me, to ensure that I returned, and also (she said) in order to face Lawrence directly, and to try and

argue him out of what he was doing, would my
father tolerate the idea of my going. But he
still insisted that I promise to return on the
Saturday night.

I told Lawrence this on the Saturday as soon as
we had all arrived (Nusch came with my mother and
me) and Lawrence was once again furious; he had
arranged at his hotel for us to spend two nights
there (we had still never had a night together)
and he felt once again that my family was trying
to come between us and boss him around. And then
my mother sat down and told him what she thought
of him, too, and what my father thought of him,
and she demanded that he simply wait and allow the
divorce, if that was what was going to happen
next, to go through. She also asked did he have
any money to support me. And all he could say was
what he had told me - that he was waiting to be
paid for the publication of his most recent novel.
But he had almost nothing else. She insisted that
he ought then to return to England and wait.

As it was impossible that I could stay with him
overnight, Lawrence decided himself to leave Trier
immediately to go up to the Rheinland, where he
would not have to pay for his food and
accommodation, though this was awkward with the
hotel which was unhappy about his canceling a
reservation. But there was nothing else I felt I
could do without alienating my parents; and I was
anyway still not sure of Lawrence, at all. In
Trier, however, later in the morning we managed at
least to walk out of the town into a bit of
country; and there behind a wall Lawrence made
love to me in a dry ditch we found: I took my hat
and my coat off and he brushed me down very
carefully and desiringly afterwards! At least
that was something. And something, as Lawrence
said, is always better than nothing.

Then we raced back into town, where I had
promised to meet my mother at the Porta Nigra at
one o'clock. But I couldn't find it, and it got
later and later, until Lawrence found it for me at

the last minute before running to catch his own train at two o'clock; so that was, for the moment the end of our escapade. And I thought it really might be the end, too.

But much worse was to come. The next day a letter from Ernst arrived in Metz saying that he refused any idea of a compromise, because "we are not rabbits", and that he was at once moving the children to London to live with his parents. This worried me a lot and I asked myself whether I should not go back to England at once, but both Nusch and Else had now gone home and could not advise me; and Lawrence was in Waldbroel, leaving me "in the lurch", as I told him. And my parents both refused to talk to me about Lawrence.

Ernst also demanded that I help him with the divorce, otherwise he might lose his Professorship and our children would starve. I thought this a bit absurd but it showed me how desperate he was feeling, which also worried me; he might do anything.

And then, a couple of days later, a letter to my mother came from him, demanding that I stop writing to him (I had only written twice, I think) or he would kill himself and the children too, and saying that I had no rights any more. This meant, I assumed, that I had no rights to see the children, and no right to any money, either. I was sure that he must be wrong about the children.

Spitefully, to show Lawrence how angry I was with him for what he had done, and to show that I was still perfectly independent of him, and did not depend on him when deciding what to do, or who to go to bed with, I wrote and told him I was thinking of having an affair with Udo von Henning, an old flame, before I left Metz; and I did go to Henning's lodgings in the center of town and encouraged him to make love to me, in the hope that it would dull my feelings of anger and misery about everything else. Lawrence compared it in a letter to "a dose of morphia", I remember, and said that he would understand if I chose to take

such a dose. That rather annoyed me:
understanding was not at all what I wanted.

Lawrence in turn wrote that his cousin Hannah was
falling in love with him, but I did not much care.
I was also starting to wonder if I were pregnant;
I had thought it impossible, but I had taken no
precautions with Lawrence and Tante Rosa was late.
One more thing to worry about.

However, that was how matters rested. More and more was I conscious that Lawrence had damaged me terribly badly, by making me send that "GANZ RECENT" telegram. I would never have done it, on my own, I would have hung on until things seemed clearer. Getting that telegram had made Ernst decide to move not just the children but the whole of our household to London; he was intending to leave me no place in the family home any more.

I also did not know how much of what Ernst was saying was threat or hysteria (his saying he would kill himself, for example, or how even seeing my handwriting made him tremble "like an old cripple", or that he was determined never to see me again) and I could not tell what he might do or really intended. I felt quite helpless. I had wanted my marriage to change, but not like this. It was all so sudden, too. I wondered whether I should not go back and see Ernst and try to stop what was happening; except that it looked as if he would refuse to see me, or even allow me into the house, and at least in Germany I had my parents and my sisters.

To make matters worse, Lawrence had also written and posted his letter to Ernst saying that he loved me and that I was with him: solid proof of the kind which Ernst would never forgive or forget, where a telegram message might have been explained. Else had told Lawrence not to write that letter, and I had too, but he had insisted. The fact that he had had to leave Metz, under duress from my father, had made it seem even more urgent to him; he had wanted to do something himself, above all he wanted to make it impossible for me to go back, he wanted me. That the only good thing in the whole mess; that I was desperately wanted by a man who was determined to become my partner, and also wanted to marry me, though I was equally determined not to marry him. I had had quite enough of marriage for the moment. But now he was hundreds of miles away and in no position to help me.

What would have struck me as comic, in another situation, was that he had written to Ernst very much under the influence of the things which I had shown him in Otto's letters. He had told Ernst, for example, that I was a giantess, and that I would smash my way through everything to get what I wanted. It was rather nice to hear that said (I had copied some of Lawrence's draft into my diary) though whether Ernst would have taken such things seriously, I very much doubt. I didn't feel at that moment at all like a giantess, or powerful in any way.

Lawrence also insisted to Ernst that I must be allowed to live my own life, but I knew that Ernst would never agree to the idea that, as a married woman, I should or could do any such thing. He was not like Edgar Jaffe, who was prepared for Else to have a child by another man, and bring it up as his own; he was not even like Max von Schreibershofen, who was so unfaithful himself that he scarcely had time to notice what Nusch was doing, or the men she was taking as lovers.

Ernst was simply old-fashioned. He demanded loyalty and the fulfilment of our church-given vows: otherwise he was intending to leave me nothing at all, just the end of our marriage.

I felt unhappy and tearful, and very much in need of sympathy. In desperation I decided to leave Metz earlier than I had said, in order to go down to Wolfratshausen to see Else and to discuss the situation. Lawrence would have to come and find me there, if he wanted to. I even began to wonder if I would ever see him again. He might well by now think me too much of a problem!

Down in Bavaria, at least, I could be surrounded by Else's children, and listen to their childish concerns, so much more important to them than anything else in the world (that helped put things in a kind of perspective). And Else, I knew, liked and rather admired Lawrence, though she knew that he had been terribly impulsive, but also understood that it had been because he wanted me.

   She could also see, clearer than me at this
stage, how determined Lawrence was to make any
retreat back into my marriage impossible. He was
being selfish and quite brutal, but at least that
showed what he wanted. And that too was
something. But the strength of his feelings in a
way frightened me; he said that he could not live
without me, that he would die without me (he had
nearly died, of pneumonia, the previous winter).
Such men, he and Ernst, both threatening to die!
Lawrence said that I was his only future. Well,
that was perhaps just as well, because it was
starting to look as if I had no other future, any
more.

14

Following advice from Else, around this time I
again wrote to Ernst about a compromise, in which
I would come back to England but would live with
his parents and the girls – or something like
that. I knew that Lawrence would have hated that
idea, but I offered it. The idea of a divorce
frightened me horribly. I felt that I would have
to go back to England, and face the judge and
plead for my rights.

I wrote very angrily to Lawrence, who was still
away with his relations up in Waldbroel. I told
him how stupid it had been of him to send that
letter to Ernst, and about how scared I was now.
He however told me not to think of doing any such
thing as going to London: "it would make you ill",
he wrote. But he also wanted me to settle things
with Ernst: by which he meant, end my marriage.
At this stage I am sure he was not thinking about
my children; he just assumed that I would be able
to go on seeing them when I went back to England.
I was still more than a bit anxious, but I also
remained sure that Ernst would be decent.

But after he had been away for almost exactly two
weeks, Lawrence came down to Muenchen; and we went
together down to a peasant inn in Beuerberg, for
what Lawrence insisted on calling our honeymoon
(he referred to us to landlords and landladies as
married: I always rebelled against that). But we
had a marvelous time; the place was a dream of
spring. We confronted terrible problems; Lawrence
wrote a poem about how our first night together
was what he called "a failure". He came so
quickly, and I got very little enjoyment. But
then he went on to write about the whole time in
his writing about Gilbert Noon, with me as
Johanna, to whom he gave our Beuerberg and Icking
life; so, again, I don't feel I need to write it
all out, less well (though where that little novel
got to, I am not sure).

But first Beuerberg and then Icking made all the
difference to us. What I remember more than

anything are the awful rows we had, with tender
love-making and wonderful excursions into the
country together in between: Lawrence was a
marvelous companion, he knew the natural world so
well. And though I was coming to love him quite a
lot, what he felt for me was much more
complicated: a rather desperate physical need
combined with a peculiar loneliness and desire to
remain independent of me, which I never really
understood. I would remind him of his assertion
that he said he would die if I left him, and he
hated that. But in a way I feared it was true; he
had told me how his father drank, and how at times
when he was engaged to the Louie Burrows girl he
had drunk himself into forgetfulness, and knew
that he could make a habit of doing that. I felt
so much less complicated than that; men are so
self-consciously tragic, Ernst and Lawrence both!
And we argued about the children all the time.

  I should explain that we moved up to Icking, to
Alfred Weber's flat, after our week in Beuerberg;
we could stay there until Alfred came. So now we
at least had somewhere to live, until August; and
I had Else within walking distance. This was not
altogether to Lawrence's liking; he regarded Else
as an enemy, because she was on the side of my
continuing marriage. But she and I both hoped
that Ernst would calm down a bit, and then we
could reach an arrangement.

  There came a letter to me from Ernst saying: "I
would have died for you." This annoyed Lawrence.
"Those phrases!" he said scornfully: "you can't
die for anybody, we each have to do our own dying
and living too." Ernst also said that he would
have spilled his blood on every paving stone in
Nottingham, for me, if I had wanted it, rather
than lose me. It was no good my answering that I
didn't want it. He felt more and more hysterical
to me (Else was right about that), and I feared
very much for Monty, who was still having to live
with him, though I know that Mrs. Kipping had
offered Monty a room in their house. But there

was nothing I could do.

What decided things for the moment was Lawrence's utter lack of money. He was expecting some money for his novel The Trespasser and was working away tremendously hard on his new one, Paul Morel he called it. But we had nothing else. It was Else who told us that we ought to go to Italy, as life was so much cheaper there, and the idea took hold of both of us. I had never really been, only to Ascona, and Lawrence had always wanted to go. Else told us how beautiful the Lago di Garda was, and that seemed a wonderful goal - and there were beautiful places on the way there, like Merano and Trento. And we could travel by walking most of the way, sending our luggage ahead. Just so as to spend the autumn in Italy, where it would be warm too; and then I could go back and see what I could sort out with Ernst.

Lawrence was especially keen on this idea; I understood that he thought that, the far side of the Alps, he would be more secure of me, and that I could not run away from him! He saw me as a reluctant pony who would have to be fastened behind the cart carrying him away, over the Alps. Though for my part I was still not at all sure that I ought to be going: it felt as if I were abandoning my children. But then I told myself that it was just for two or three months at most, that I couldn't go back and see them for the moment anyway, but in a couple of months Ernst would have calmed down and then I could go back and we could find how the children and I were going to live, in the future.

"I have done with you, I want to forget you and
you must be dead to the children. You know the
law is on my side." Those were the terrible words
which Ernst suddenly wrote to me, towards the end
of December: an agonizing moment. All the autumn,
in Gargnano, I had been writing to him and I
thought negotiating with him about my return to
England and how and where I might see the children
again (Monty was now twelve, Elsa ten, Barbara had
just had her eighth birthday in October: I had
written to her but doubt if she ever got my
letter).

And for months too I had been getting letters
from Ernst: madly accusing, pleading, offering,
denouncing, which I had always attempted to answer
sensibly. He had, to begin with, suggested that
if I returned to England, in order to sustain a
vestige of respectability he would allow me to see
the children. And then he demanded that if I
would go back to live with my parents, in Metz,
and did not see other men, then after a year – but
what followed was unclear. And then, late in the
autumn, providing that I gave Lawrence up, he had
actually offered me a flat in London with access
to the children (though it was unclear whether he
would also have access to the flat, or whether I
would have to live with him "Altogether as his
wife" – even if not "at first").

Such an offer, which I told my family about, and
which depended on my giving Lawrence up, made my
family certain that I must accept it! Else wrote
to Lawrence at the start of December telling him
that though she believed he had behaved
heroically, he must now sacrifice himself for the
happiness of me and the children, by giving me up,
by going back to England and resolving not to see
me again.

And Lawrence refused. He showed me what he
wrote to Else, and it was about sacrifice – and
how my giving him up now (if I did) would actually
burden the children, later on. "The worst of

67

sacrifice is that we have to pay back", he read to me. The children would have to make it up to me, what I had sacrificed for them; that was his theory.

And he insisted on staying with me. And really I did not want to go back into my marriage with Ernst. I wanted a new life. And though life with Lawrence had been so troubled, over and over again, I also loved living as the companion of a writer and seeing the pages mounting up, ready for me to read (Ernst had never showed me anything). For the moment, life with Lawrence was better than anything I was likely to get away from him. I could always change things later, I thought.

And there was the simple matter of money. I had nothing from Ernst, of course; my parents certainly could not afford to keep me, nor could Else support me in the future. And though my sister Nusch would give me presents when she could, there was nothing ever to be relied on. I had brought myself unthinkingly to depend on Lawrence, just for everyday living. There was no way I could ever get work in the out-of-the-way places where he wanted to write!

And I was still sure I would see the children again before long, though I knew it might now be a bit longer. I had at first hoped for some time before Christmas, then at latest by Easter; "I could never be quite hard on a woman", Ernst had written to me. That meant a lot to me.

But, by December, Ernst was writing less. Things had altered over the months. It turned out that he had decided that he was going to divorce me. And that was the end, he had decided. No more hanging about, no more uncertainty. And he would not be writing to me again; so I would hear nothing more about the children either.

And there I was in Gargnano, utterly miserable, living with a man who refused to understand what I was feeling, but on whom I was entirely dependent, lacking even the money to go back to Germany. I knew why he refused to understand. He of all men, the writer of that great mother-demolishing book Sons and Lovers, was in dread of the power of a woman and the damage she could do to her children. He simply could not collaborate with my desire to have my children, no matter what. He knew that it was a choice: either him or them. And he wanted me. So he did not want the children, and could not suffer with me, or even sympathize in my feelings.

I went down to the lake late one winter evening, after he had gone to bed and was asleep. The waves were lapping, gently swishing at my feet. I felt so flayed myself, my misery was like a shameful disease to me. I had always known how to be bright and cheerful, even if I did not feel so. Now I was utterly alone, and miserable. I wanted to hide, to creep away from things. The water was licking my feet rhythmically. I imagined how, slowly, mechanically, I would take off my things, my boots, my underclothes. I wanted to be one of those stones under the clear, protecting water. I would creep into the water. Slowly I would sit down, slipping into the shallow water gradually, slipping deeper and deeper. Now the waves would touch my breast; I would catch my breath, then the waves would go over me gently lapping. My arms and legs would relax, I would sink back in the water.

That was how I imagined it and what I wrote, years later: a fantasy of how miserable I had been in Gargnano, and what I might easily have done with myself, because of the children being taken from me.

But I talked myself out of it; I went on, knowing that in the spring life would change.

It did not, of course. Ernst never wrote, and
Lawrence insisted on staying, first in Italy, and
then in Bavaria, in my brother-in-law's little
wooden house. Finally back in the summer, in
England, first David Garnett (Edward's son) and
then Katherine Mansfield tried to help me see the
girls at St Paul's School; at least I got a
message to them via Monty. And I saw them in the
street, on their way to school. I watched the
house in Chiswick for hours (I had discovered it
by looking for my Nottingham curtains, and had
found them). And then I tried again, and actually
walked into the house one evening, when they were
having their tea in the kitchen, as usual. But
the moment I came in the kitchen door, a young
woman (I guess one of Ernst's family) jumped up
and shoved me out, and I hardly saw the children
at all, just their astonished faces. I hoped
that, after that, they would plead to be allowed
to see me, now that I had shown them how close I
was and how I wanted to be with them. But nothing
came; they must have been prevented. And a court
order was placed on me (or was that the previous
year?) But I had seen them; they were still
alive, though they had grown so much!

In fact, as I feared, my life as I was extracted
from my first marriage, and lost touch with my
children, got much harder, not easier. I saw
Ernst just once, in all these years: that was in
the winter of 1914, when I went to Nottingham with
Lawrence. Without telling him what I was going to
do, I called at the house in town where Ernst had
his lodgings (the address was in the Directory)
and had myself announced by the German-sounding
landlady as "Mrs. Lawson" – and was immediately
shown into his study. Ernst backed away from me
when he saw me: "You . . . I hoped never to see
you again . . . what are you doing in this town?
Do you want to drive me off the face of the earth,
woman? Is there no place where I can have peace?"
He asked whether I was not ashamed to show my face

where I was known – and then fell to insulting me: "Isn't the commonest prostitute better than you?" I simply said, over and over again, that I had to talk to him about the children. Eventually he rounded on me: "You shall <u>not</u> have them – they don't want to see you . . . my solicitors have instructions to arrest you, if you attempt to interfere with them." I told him I didn't care. But by then he had rung for his landlady, and with her in the room he insisted that I leave or the police would be called and eventually I did leave, wanting to cry but determined not to show it. And then I heard and saw no more for months and months, and my heart ached and ached.

By then I had married Lawrence. This was something I had sworn never to do but Lawrence had talked to Edward Marsh and was convinced that a European War was almost certainly going to start, and he was worried what might happen to me if I were not married (Ernst had divorced me); Lawrence believed that I would be interned, as an enemy alien. In that he was almost certainly right. So we got married, in July 1914, from Campbell's house in Kensington. There are pictures showing us on the wedding day, and one of me in my wedding dress.

But the following summer, when we were stuck in England because of the War, and living in Hampstead, word suddenly came from Ernst's solicitors that, on 11 August, I could see the children in their office for thirty minutes. This was when we had money, this big advance from the publisher of <u>The Rainbow</u>, and after I had insisted to Lawrence that I needed to live in London, and he had promised me a little flat of my own; but he had chosen one a long way from Chiswick. It was, however, a kind of separation; and the money meant that we could afford to live apart. But while he was still down in Sussex, and I was in London, I had again spent hours hanging around St Paul's School, and Elsa and Barbara had seen me. I now think it possible that <u>they</u> had asked Ernst to be allowed to see me. The fact my birthday was chosen certainly suggests that the visit was some kind of a present.

Seeing them was extraordinary: they had all changed so much (it was three years since I had seen them properly). I was not allowed to hand over to them any of the little presents I had brought - the solicitors insisted that they must take the presents and see whether Professor Weekley would allow the children to have them. But I saw their eyes sparkle and heard their voices. Monty was rather reserved, and Elsa at times looked very angrily at me. But Barby came to be hugged, just as she always had, in the old days; and all three by the end seemed to have enjoyed themselves (I had asked them so many questions about school and their achievements: about how Elsa was always top of her class, and Monty sometimes was, and how well Barby was learning to draw). Then I had to leave, and was instructed not to stay in the area, as the children's aunt would be coming to collect them, and would not do so, so long as I was there. So, again in tears, I walked away down the road to the tube station (this was in Chiswick) and found my way back to Hampstead.

But then came the disaster of the prosecution of The Rainbow, which was withdrawn and Lawrence was supposed to pay all the money back; and we had never been so poor. No more flats for me! The only thing we could do was go down to a borrowed house in Cornwall, and look for a place we could afford. But with no money, except for a few bits trickling in from Lawrence's poetry, we were obliged to stay there for almost a year before we could even afford the train fare to let me come back up to London. Ernst however now seemed to believe that he should allow me occasional access to the children. And he allowed it to happen twice more during the War, or it may have been three times (once in Mark Gertler's studio, with his wonderful paintings all around us, I recall).

So what was this life with Lawrence like? It was
not really very like the life I described in Not
I. For one thing, although he did his very best
with the small amount of money we had, and gave me
everything he could, including jewelry and
precious stones, we were mostly "out in the
sticks" because that was cheapest, but also
because Lawrence chose places where he thought he
could write, like Cornwall, or out in Berkshire.
We hardly ever lived in places where I could
manage to lead my own independent life; only at
the Mirenda much later could I take the tram into
Florence, which I did regularly. But for most of
our time together, I actually had very little to
do. I had never been any good at needlework,
though I embroidered a few things. I read books.
But Lawrence always took over the household
because that was something he understood and I
never had done. I read what he wrote and
criticized it and sometimes (when he asked) copied
it; and I did learn to cook and to make lunch for
us. I even tried typing, to see if I could, but I
could never get it right; and as usual Lawrence
was much better at it than I was, so I gave it up.

But after cur lunch we would go out and walk and
this was often the best part of the day for me,
when he talked to me and we discussed things. I
noticed how, when we had people to stay (they were
always his friends, in England I didn't have any
English friends who would still come and see me)
that was when our untroubled way of life got most
broken up and we both got unhappy and quarreled
much worse than when we were quietly on our own.
But our quarrels were exhausting and long. He had
a terrible temper which at times drove him over
the edge of sanity. His black moods, accumulating
in blackness, would take him over. I did not know
where they came from, everything seemed drowned in
blackness and I was helpless. I could not escape.
We were too aware of each other. "No woman could
stand this" I thought to myself. I did not bear

him a grudge, I knew it was part of his make-up, but he seemed helpless, given over to blackness, and out of that he seemed to enjoy torturing me too. I was many times frightened though never the last bit of me; but at times he hit me, really lashed out and hurt me. I am no angel of light myself; sometimes out of sheer exasperation I hit him (I once smashed a stone plate over his head). But once, I remember, he had worked himself up and his hands were on my throat and he was pressing me against the wall and grinding out "I am the master, I am the master." I said "Is that all? You can be master as much as you like, I don't care." He dropped his hands, he looked at me in astonishment, and was all right, that time. We nearly parted though, more than once: on one occasion he counted out on to the table our entire store of money, in sovereigns, and divided them up between us, as a preliminary to my leaving.

But though I sometimes really wanted to go, I could never do so; during the War I could not leave England, and the only people who would have accepted me into their houses were Lawrence's friends, like the Carswells. There was no-one in Nottingham who would have taken me in. Later on, someone like Mabel Luhan in Taos would perhaps have taken me in; but I did not like her. And I never had a penny of my own, not until shortly before Lawrence died; but I was not going to demean myself, washing bottles or something like that. I would rather have drowned myself, as I had thought about in Gargnano.

As a German person, too, I was (during the War) always the object of suspicion and sometimes of actual anger. I had to stick with Lawrence, though it was often very hard indeed to accept that that way of life was what my life had been reduced to. But that was how it was. In the War, too, not only could I hear very little about my children, I could hear nothing from my family either. It was months before I even heard about the death of my father, for example. It was an awful time; and at the end we had to wait and wait before we could get passports. I was not able to leave for nearly nine months after the War was over; and found my mother in a very bad state, with almost no money. It was Lawrence who had sometimes to come to her rescue: the collier's son supporting the aristocrat. That was something new for the Richthofens.

But after the War we could at least travel again, and what a relief that was; down to Sicily, for example, while I could also go back and stay with my mother in Baden-Baden, sometimes for weeks at a time. I was simply aware of time passing by, and the twenty-first birthdays of my children all gradually approaching, and I wondered how they would react to me after all the years that had passed.

Lawrence, though, remained as angry about my love for my children as he always had been. Looking back, I do not think it can have been an accident that, when Monty became twenty-one and I had (I thought cleverly) arranged to be in Germany with my mother that summer, hoping that Monty might take the chance of visiting his grandmother, Lawrence grew especially angry about my family and made remarks like "relatives are a mistake, one should never see one's relations – or anybody else's". And before Elsa became twenty-one, he decided we should take our chance to go to India to see the Brewsters and then to go on, round the world, and we stayed in Australia and New Mexico and it was pretty well as far away from the children as we could have got.

Finally I persuaded him that we had to go back to Europe – and as our American visas were expiring, he agreed. But that led to the biggest quarrel of our married life; I shall come to that.

What was life like with Lawrence, by then? You, Betsy, will have noticed that I have not been talking about sex much, over the last few weeks when I have been dictating. That was because sex did not play much of a part in our lives either.

Back at the time when we first met, I had to teach him how to be a good lover, and he learned a bit, and could come more than once, though he was never very interested in satisfying me. And the first time he usually came too quickly to be much good to me; but at times it was good. It was during the War that he, like Ernst, developed a desire to take me from behind, and not just from behind, and we did it a few times. But it was nothing to me; just useful a bit for him in his writing, I think, and in helping him understand homosexual people like Whitman; at least I guess it did.

But his passion for me, which had led him to all his demands and insistence at the start, and to his saying things like "I would die if you left me", that died down. Sex became just occasional; it became the way he described it in his novel Kangaroo, when the Lawrence man makes love to his wife after being in the sea, and it is a bit surprising to her, but she quite likes it. That was how sex was for me; something I partly forgot about, but never really forgot.

And then, a few years before Lawrence died, came Ravagli, whom I really enjoyed and who made love like a good Italian; so that after all those years I had a passionate lover again, much to my astonishment.

But coming back to Lawrence: what mattered very
much to me, however, was the way that between 1913
and 1926 I would find myself the real woman behind
character after character in his works of fiction.
This is my riches, my glory. My deepest
conviction and happiness is that I was part of his
work as I was of his life. This was one of the
things which showed me that he was still
interested in me. I am Elsa ("a handsome woman,
large, blonde, about 30") in his play The Married
Man, written I remember soon after he met me: but
I was not that fat at the time. There I am, too,
singing in an early fragment of "The Sisters",
"Her idea of time was sketchy, but she had a
strong, rather beautiful voice." Ernst too had
criticized my keeping of time, but I never noticed
it. And then I became Ursula in both The Rainbow
and Women in Love. I get so easily puffed up when
I read them: it's me, it's me, so much is me!
That scene where I throw the ring at him; that
happened. Then I appear as Paula ("a beautiful
woman of about thirty, fair, luxuriant, with proud
shoulders and a face borne up by a fierce, native
vitality") in his story "New Eve and Old Adam",
before the War. I do like those shoulders and
that vitality! I am certainly Elsa in the Dowson
story "The Overtone", also Marta ("Her dark-blond
hair was gathered loosely . . . her young,
blossom-fresh face was lifted") in "The Mortal
Coil", and in Aaron's Rod Tanny ("strong and
fair"). Lawrence first wrote "a fine blonde" but
I substituted "strong and fair" in pencil, I
remember that Thomas Seltzer accepted my
substitution, but Secker did not. I am Johanna
("fair and fresh-faced and just over thirty") in
Mr. Noon, Hannele again ("a fair woman with dark-
blond hair and a beautiful fine skin") in The
Captain's Doll, Harriett ("a mature, handsome,
fresh-faced woman") in Kangaroo, Katharine ("a
handsome woman of forty, no longer slim, but
attractive in her soft, feminine way") in "The

Border-Line", finally Kate ("a beautiful woman, in her own unconventional way, and with a certain richness. She was going to be forty next week") in The Plumed Serpent.

These are portraits, but not just still-life portraits. They are women who are looking for something more in their lives, just like me. They are real adventuresses, if I can call them that. In those ways my life went to the making of Lawrence's work; without me in his life, he would never have written such things, nor developed such theories about sex and the unconscious. It was while I was the love-inspiration for his work that it was at its best, I am sure; I am not the only reader who found Sons and Lovers and The Rainbow and Women in Love the best of his writing.

But all the novels he wrote, certainly down to The Plumed Serpent, but also even Lady Chatterley, might also count as ways of updating the story of my life, not just my appearance, as seen by an incomparable artist. The unfinished fragment "The Woman who Wanted to Disappear" was perhaps Lawrence's last refashioning of me, in 1929, in the last piece of fiction he ever wrote. And there were other writings of his drawing indirectly upon reminiscences of life with me, such as the character (though not the appearance) of Anita in the story "Once—!". I could also add all the essential experiences of the character (though not the appearance or the family history) of Connie in Lady Chatterley (there Lawrence looked back at our early sexual history and wrote about it very beautifully, if not really very accurately).

With such writing constantly recreating me, at first I felt no need to write my own life story, either then or later on, after Lawrence's death. My unfolding and developing life had been drawn out for me, in ways which no-one really saw or understood but me, and far more brilliantly than I could ever have done it. But as Lawrence read these works aloud to me in the evenings, I could see him judging the accuracy of his portraits, and his development of the characters, and making corrections to what he had written, as he found that his writing and my reality did not exactly coincide. I felt responsible for what he wrote; I felt myself involved in the creation.

But we went on quarreling over the children. Once, at the ranch in New Mexico in the 1920s, he actually tore up one of the few photographs I had of them, that was the cruelest thing he ever did to me, and I hated him for that. He also tried to stop me sending them letters, which I always wanted to do for their birthdays. He did this at the ranch, I know, he dug into the heap of letters put out for the postman.

19

But the strangest thing of all then happened to us
in the autumn and winter of 1923. We had had that
terrible disagreement in New York in August, when
after everything had been arranged, the steamer
tickets bought, and we had come to New York, at
the last minute he had refused to come with me to
Europe, and I had none-the-less insisted on going.
The reason I was so determined was that I knew I
would legally be able to see Monty and Elsa, Monty
having had his twenty-first birthday a couple of
years before, and Elsa being about to have hers,
on 13 September. That was my real reason for
absolutely insisting on coming to England; not as
Lawrence's partner, but so as to recover my
children. And Lawrence knew this, and hated it:
Murry told me how he wrote from New York something
horrible like "I can't stomach chasing those
Weekley children". He was refusing to see them as
my children. He wrote me letters to England, one
after another, but never once mentioned the
children, just said he hated the thought of
personalities (he meant my love for my children, I
was sure) and that he hated the thought of England
– and of Germany even more.
    It was the first time in our marriage that we had
parted not knowing where or how or even whether we
would see each other again. Even back in 1919,
when we were apart for more than six weeks, and I
was visiting my family in Germany, with
communications by post almost impossible, we knew
we would eventually be meeting in Florence.
    However in 1923 I came to London and saw many of
our old friends and saw both children, especially
Monty. That was marvelous: he was so handsome!
And so clever too; Murry met him and was very
impressed. I was still in no doubt that Lawrence
would eventually come; I took it for granted. He
however spent months aridly travelling in Mexico
with our painter friend Goetzsche, and he wrote to
me as if he believed we would not be living
together again. He made all kinds of financial

arrangements for me, for example.

This might have given me a clue but I confess that it did not, not yet. This was, incidentally, when I was also drawn to Murry and felt like starting an affair with him, but found that he had decided to occupy the moral high ground, and refused, wanting to be "loyal to Lorenzo", as he put it. Jack always took things too seriously and too morally; he would not have been the first lover I had had during my marriages. Being committed to Lawrence did not prevent me from having, every now and then, affairs (I am thinking of men like Hobson or Garnett). I could love them for an evening or an afternoon, though not usually for a night. And in no way had such sudden times of mutual love and happiness detracted from my everyday life with Lawrence or from what in the end was I think even more important, my devotion to his genius. They were simply happy episodes, to be valued especially as I got older.

Lawrence was sometimes aware of these passionate excursions (very little escaped him), and he had once or twice got angry about them, but he had never attempted to stop me, or had apparently thought of leaving me (or was apparently prepared for me to leave him), until this time during the autumn of 1923. He may have suspected that something was going on between me and Murry but I am also confident that he never thought that it could be serious; he knew he could not lose me to Murry. But eventually in December he came back to England, I can only suppose in a kind of admission that, in spite of the children, he found that he could not do without me.

When however he arrived in London, he immediately and rather strangely fell ill. It was not just that his arid time in Mexico had dried something out of him; there was another reason. For the first time I instinctively felt that he was a man now always destined to be ill, and whose health I could no longer set right except at moments. He had become strange to me. And this was, I thought, because I had at last started to recover my children (I would get Barby back in 1925), and realized instinctively that I did not want this sick man Lawrence too. It was as if he knew this; knew that I was unconsciously deciding this: had actually known it back in New York, which was why he had not wanted me to go, and would not come himself, and had argued with me about it so strenuously. And now I had the children. He had always feared that he would lose me, which was why at times he spoke so witheringly about "those Weekley children". He refused to admit that they were mine, that they were the children I had left for him. Now I was leaving him for them. Or that was what he felt. And he was right: he was lost to me.

And this period broke his organic kind of dependence upon me. He had always been jealous of the children, but now it became a brief, passionate jealousy. In the spring after I had seen Monty and Elsa, we went back together to the USA, to the ranch, and here he committed himself to months of physical effort, as he helped re-build the ranch at Kiowa; he worked under the roofs in the heat and dust, doing everything our Indian laborers did, sparing himself nothing which they did. This was his attempt to make the permanent home which I had always craved and where we could spend our lives together, away from London and from my children. But he also wanted to show me (as he had done in his long walking holidays before the War) that he was still a radiantly well man, a fitting partner to me and my triumphant good health.

It was almost his last attempt. After all the
work was successfully done, and while he was
recovering, and writing those American stories
like St. Mawr, he had his first awful hemorrhage,
in August 1924. It was exactly as if the illness
came because, in spite of everything he had done,
he knew he had all the same lost me, and I would
never settle here in America so long as Barby and
the others were in Europe and I believed needed
me.

He made one more attempt, back in Europe, when
he started to write Lady C and involved me in
remembering all our very earliest sexual
encounters, and what I had felt. But it was all
reminiscent, none of it was actual; he felt no
desire for me, that I knew, in spite of the way in
which his writing those episodes was, I was sure,
a way of trying to provoke desire. Under the
influence of what he was writing he even attempted
to make love to me again, more than once, but he
could do very little physically: he lacked the
desire. He could only turn his face towards
death. And then started the long, sad slope down
to the end; and all I could do was watch him go,
and help where I could.

It was not as if I was in love with him any
more. What love we had had, in for example
Fiascherino before the War, when he was writing
The Rainbow and I had felt buoyed up by his love
for me into feeling deeply for him as he toiled
over the novel, and fought with Garnett, and
toiled over it again: that was something
unexpected. I was aware of his dependence on me,
but, looking back, I now believe that this was the
first time that I really loved him too. This came
to an end, in Sussex I think, in the first year of
the War, when I demanded to have a flat of my own
in London; and there some last shreds of love in
Cornwall, perhaps; but the love had also simply
been worn down by the hard life we had led. And
then it was just a long affection, interrupted by

terrible rows at times, but accompanied by the extraordinariness of being always his questing heroine.

And in all his work he had always had my allegiance, my absolute belief in what I thought of as the deepest Lawrence. With all my might I had also wanted him to live, and helped him. But now, when we were down in Oaxaca for example, I also knew that it was my job to help him to die as he would want to die, proud and himself. And he almost did die. It was my job to see him through that, and to ensure that he never felt like an invalid. And that I mostly managed, though he always had the most terrible and piercing insight into my states of mind, as when he told Barby, just a couple of days before he died, "your mother does not care for me any more, the death in me is repellent to her". How well he knew me; and I had tried so hard not to let him see that. But it was exactly what I felt; and I wanted to be with my new man Angie, too, who was such a support to me in those last months, as Lawrence knew. And sexually I wanted Angie, who made love to me exactly as Lawrence could only now do in his imagination. I was so proud to have a new lover. I am fairly sure that Lawrence knew about Angie from the start, but on one awful occasion he found an actual letter from Angie which my mother had sent on, and that meant a blazing row in which he was as crude and rude as he could be, and it led to his collapse into bed (this was on the Isle de la Port Cros, a rather awful time all round).

It was then left to me to write Lawrence's life in Not I, but the Wind; there is not much about me in that book, but in some ways there is not much about Lawrence either! I wrote nothing about sex, of course, but I also hid the fact of his violence and his temper, and the way we were hardly a couple any more towards the end of his life. And afterwards I started to write my own memoirs of myself – but for years I could only manage to write in fragments.

My problem was simple. Nothing I wrote could
ever match up to those constant, amazing portraits
and explorations which Lawrence had done of me in
his fiction as I grew from my thirties into
middle-age. I wanted, as he did, to grasp the
meaning of my long years, of the changes I
suffered, why I was compelled to do this thing and
not that, the out of the way places many and
varied I had seen and all the people I had cared
for — and those not cared for. And how at first,
before I met Lawrence, I had wanted to save people
from their bourgeois, repression-dominated lives,
and had been fanatic about it, and about sexual
freedom, under the influence of Otto. And I still
often think about those things, too, even though I
am now contented and peaceful leading this quiet
busy life in El Prado, just outside Taos (people
are always coming wanting to know about Lawrence).

But I was never able to do the writing I really
wanted. For one thing, Lawrence seemed to have
done it all. I always fell back on just writing,
yet again, about my childhood; my childhood was
indeed the root of everything, but it was also the
only thing that I felt remained truly my own. I
loved turning it over and over in my hands and in
the words I found for it, in the way in which one
can caress a beloved and precious object.
Lawrence had only written about a bit of it, my
time in the garden with my father, with the
asparagus, which he put into The Rainbow as
potatoes (there was not much asparagus grown in
England, that was why).

What I have learned from this long period of
talking to Betsy is different from anything I
thought before. I have understood for the first
time how my nature is still fundamentally the same
as when I was a child. A man like Ernst was not
the least able to understand this. He saw me only
as I first looked: as an immensely desirable young
woman, a sexual being, willing and waiting to be
taken sexually. He could not realize, having
grown up so quickly himself, having stopped being
a child so early out of sheer necessity, and now
being so worn down by work and by so many years of
tedious adult experience, that I was quite
different. He had not only forgotten what it was
like to be a child; he would also have believed it
quite wrong ever to go back to being one. It was
his moral duty not to be a child but to be the
adult he had become. He never, if possible, saw
me as a child either: as one who was fresher than
him, living every moment intensely in a way that
he never could, and always ready for experience.
He thought he was the one who led the way in
experience; that it was my job to follow.

He preferred to idealize me, which is the worst
of crimes in love. If ever he had had just a
glimpse of the fact that my real gift was pure,
child-like simplicity, the simplicity that takes
things exactly as they come, which lives moment
for moment, in the moment, then I believe he would
have rejected it, or would have turned it into a
love for me as a virginally pure woman (a purity
which all the same, in sex, he could not have
resisted setting out to violate).

Sex really got in the way for him. He was
furiously sensual but he never knew what my
straightforwardness meant. He would have thought
I was just immoral, if for example I had admitted
being attracted to other men, or had said I wanted
to go with them, or had indeed done so. What Otto
helped me realize is that sex is the highest thing
in life, and there is no reason to be ashamed

about it, but for Ernst it was something he did in the dark, secretly and urgently, and which only involved me as an accepting object. He never knew, but would have hated it if he had realized it, that I am a woman who lives fully in every moment, and that sex is simply one of those moments, if a long lasting one. This makes me in some ways inconsistent and disloyal, which Ernst also hated, being as he was not only a principled and conventicnally moral but also a logical and rational man.

So he got me wrong from the start. I wanted to play, like a child, and he never did. That was true from the very beginning of our marriage, for example in the hotel in Luzern. I hope that in the long run I may perhaps have influenced him into being less anxious and into making jokes even in his serious writing, which he said was his kind of play, and which he said was something he owed to me, and would not have done without me (though I am sure he forgot this as the years went by). But in only this single way was he perhaps influenced by me, and understood me better than Otto did, Otto with his eternal demands that, with my nature, I should be the outstanding and overwhelming woman of the future. Otto never saw me as a fruitful child: he only saw me as a marvelously sexual adult, the "flowering fruitful yes". It has taken me years to realize this.

But I recall too how Ernst encouraged me and helped me with those three little publications on which are the name of Frieda Weekley (and although he inscribed me as solely responsible for two of them, the poems of Schiller and the tiny book of Bechstein's Maerchen, no-one glancing at the notes at the back could be in any doubt as to who had been responsible for them). And then our Lektor in Nottinghan, Ludwig Stahl, asked me to look at his translation of a little play by Yeats, I'm not sure why, but he added my name as co-translator: he may simply have wanted the name "Weekley" somewhere on his edition, to give it reputation and what they here in the US call heft.

Ernst encouraged me in these various ventures (in fact he pushed me into them) in part because he was so proud of me, and wanted to show me off. But he also wanted to show – to himself too, perhaps – that I was not only a child, not completely child-like. He wanted to show me as, and for me to be, a serious, intellectual adult woman, and these things were the proof of it. But in reality I found such things mainly fun, interesting games to play, the way I mostly found reading Lawrence's work fun (though I must admit that there were some tough nuts to crack, in his "philosophical" writing, which I did not much enjoy).

But Lawrence loved me because he, of all these men, with his marvelous, uncanny insight, could see the way in which I was not only a sexual woman but in some ways still a child; he could not only draw on it in his writing, but he could love me because it meant so much to him that I could still be so spontaneous and be so set upon fulfilling my desires. He could love me because I was a child. He had never known anyone or anything like me.

It also annoyed him terribly at times. I never forget the awful quarrel we had in Icking, after I had bought this furry spider (metal under the fur) which I had fallen in love with in a toy-shop in Muenchen; and we were so poor, and I had stolen the money from our tiny stock of household money. But I could not be without it. And eventually he understood.

Much of what people admire in Lawrence, with his doctrines of following your instincts, he got from me. He called it insouciance, in the end, which I think meant being relaxed as an aristocrat is relaxed, happy in a position of superiority. That too he got from me!

22

For now at the end I must sing my own praises.
What I do, I do with a whole heart. Or that I
hope is what I have learned from my mistakes to
do.

I know that I did not whole-heartedly marry or
love Ernst, and that was my fault, and maybe the
problem from the start; I married him to get away
from home, and because I was bewildered by him,
and also fascinated by him as a highly
intelligent, self-believing man who always seemed
to know what he wanted, and who clearly wanted me
so much. In knowing so well what he wanted, and
working so hard to earn our living, he was so
different from my two other suitors, my Richthofen
cousin Kurt and Monbart! And that meant a great
deal.

I also believed then, as I believe now, that our
lives are essentially an adventure. And to me
England was an adventure, almost as much as
marriage was.

It was, too, with a whole heart that, in the
end, I accepted Lawrence. But that did not happen
until we had got down to the Lago di Garda for
those six awful months of exile. He wanted me to
believe that his life depended on me. My only
profound regret is the way his need for me – and
consequently his insistence on telling Ernst the
truth about us – had led to Ernst's far too hasty
decision to abandon our marriage. It led directly
to my loss of my children.

Ernst, sadly, never awoke me to a sense of what
I might be, which was not only to be a housewife
in Nottingham: nor simply the woman he wanted to
sleep with: nor really a wife at all, inevitably
the servant of others, with children depending on
her. He did not want a woman who could just be
herself, richly and independently, enjoying her
own sensuality, having men when she wanted them,
and provoking a man to write more deeply than any
other writer of his generation. That, I
eventually discovered, was my role in life.

For I was the person for whom Lawrence was
waiting, demanding as he did that I should love
him and go away with him. He wanted me to serve
his genius, but I also knew at once how much as a
writer he needed me. Freud, as Otto had made
clear to me, would be a clue to so much which
Lawrence needed to understand. He was already a
marvelous writer, but I knew I could show him what
I was like, as an instinctive woman, as the woman
of the future I believed myself to be. That would
be something for him! I could liberate him from
his problems with women: I could educate him into
what Freud said about repressed feelings and their
consequences; and he could learn especially about
sons loving their mothers.

But it turned out that something else was even
more important. I could also make him realize
what it was like to live fully and spontaneously
in every moment, as he had never himself done -
and then have him write about it, for the sake of
his contemporaries.

I realized I could do this for him. I did not
think of myself as his wife; I would be his muse.

But I also wanted my children. Hence our
terrible quarrels. He thought I could not have
him and them. I wanted both, even if I failed.
But I am so grateful, now, first in an odd way to
Ernst, and then to Otto, most of all to Lawrence
and finally to Angelo. If today I am a free
woman, with still loving children, it is because
these men in their very different ways supported
me. Lawrence earned the money on which I now
live. Angelo has made the conditions of life in
North America possible for me by taking care of
me, even if he has sometimes to look for another
woman. (Yes, keep that in.)

What, however, none of these men apart from
Lawrence knew and accepted - though Angie has a
faint, unthinking sense of it - is that I am at
bottom profoundly matter-of-fact, accepting events
as they are given. This is actually what I mean
by being aristocratic: accepting that things are

as they are. Idealism (meaning attempting to change things) does not interest me at all; political and ethical systems are only of passing interest to me. Instead, in old age I am lucky enough to experience the ripeness of my at last completed childhood. A friend wrote about me, let me boast here too, that I possess "a certain native aristocracy". That speaks to me; it feels like me. I am not just an old-fashioned aristocrat, that says so little, there are so many stupid ones. But in myself I am one naturally: or so I believe. That was **xxxxx** also what Lawrence loved in me.

Anyhow I have achieved all that and a thought comes, then another the very opposite, but often I **xxxxx** just go on in a secretly joyful way, as if I did not want people to know how happy I am. For Ernst's death means that my old grounds for hate and suffering are gone, and I feel released into "the pursuit of happiness". Old though I am, I know that I have this one thing to do; to leave a faithful record. So I have told the story of young Frieda. No other title or name is necessary for me, which might define me in relation to this man or that man. Definition never takes account of the glamour in life. I knew this with Lawrence. And I believe that as Young Frieda, I am forever young.

Frieda Lawrence Ravagli

~~89~~ 91

inside these covers are works of fiction which draw upon and at times quote actual documents, but are primarily concerned with filling in the gaps around the facts. Documentary evidence, so far as it is known, is never altered or ignored, although it is constantly supplemented (though slightly normalised): the two books are as truthful as I can manage. No quotation marks have, however, been used when documentary material has been cited: everything factual here demands its share of marital rights with the fictional, everything fictional has been married to the documentary. All biographies of Frieda Lawrence are hopelessly flawed by the lack of evidence from the years of her first marriage, to Ernest Weekley; there has, too, never been a full length biography of Weekley. What he was like, what Frieda's marriage was like, how and why she carried it on for thirteen years, how and why she turned to D. H. Lawrence – from the evidence, these things can only be guessed at or ignored, after brief speculation. I once attempted to write a biography of Frieda, and was unable to solve the problem of how to write about the years of her marriage to Weekley; so abandoned what I had written. The two narratives

A ROMANCE:

WITH WORDS

BY ERNEST WEEKLEY, M . A.

SOMETIME PROFESSOR OF FRENCH AND HEAD OF THE MODERN LANGUAGE DEPARTMENT AT
UNIVERSITY COLLEGE, NOTTINGHAM; SOMETIME SCHOLAR OF TRINITY COLLEGE, CAMBRIDGE;
AUTHOR OF "THE ROMANCE OF WORDS", "SURNAMES"

"On est aisément dupé par ce qu'on aime."

(MOLIÈRE, *Le Tartuffe*, iv. 3.)

LONDON

1939

PREFACE

This volume is offered to those who, in the past, have been kind enough to show interest in my books on the strange but fascinating developments of etymology. It is an attempt to explain something of the life of the individual who has been surveying that field for so many years with such closeness of attention; and, as with all such first attempts, it will doubtless be found not only lacking in many respects but its date of completion will, I fear, have a way of receding the closer it is approached. I am however now near to my seventy-fifth birthday, and if I do not embark upon the attempt in some haste (though, as John Wesley counsels, 'never in a hurry') it might indeed prove pointless, the results being doomed to the waste-paper basket by harassed executors.

A further provocation to write comes in the form of the warnings of forthcoming war. If it were to come then I should have only intellectual internment in Criccieth to look forward to, without my library, though in the company of my friends the great scientist Professor Stanley Kipping and his wife. This book would at least require less recourse to a library than any other book for which I have been responsible.

I have in fact been considering over the last seven years how to respond to a volume I acquired in 1931: a short novel entitled *The Virgin and the Gipsy*. The book was apparently published (in

iii

Florence) just three months after its author, the wretched and, I believe, in the end miserably unhappy writer D. H. Lawrence had succumbed to consumption. He had first come to my notice when the world proclaimed him a young genius: I cannot resist noting that he left it a notorious pornographer, the *Daily Telegraph* commemorating him in its obituary notice as one who wrote 'with one hand always in the slime'. It was a short obituary but must have been written by 'one who perfectly well knew the captain'.

The Virgin and the Gipsy had been published with a dedication: necessarily the last of Lawrence's many books (many times too many, some may say) to be dedicated. The reason for the dedication is not far to seek: the name given was the name of his wife. A different light may, however, be cast upon the dedication when readers realise that the novel contains a portrait of that very woman, almost undisguised, as a wife named Cynthia, 'glamorous but not very dependable', who for no particular reason leaves her first husband and family for a younger man: the abandoned 'base-born' husband being a corrupt and untrustworthy clergyman called Saywell, a name which I suspect Lawrence of finding in my own book *Surnames*: I am flattered that he should have got as far as page 254.

And here I must venture upon the kind of personal admission with which, like Wordsworth, I do not often delight to season my fireside or my conversation. Saywell is an even more slightly disguised and probably, if I chose to pursue the matter, libellous portrait of me. The story which follows centres on the vulgar but rather unconvincing romance of Saywell's younger daughter Yvette with a gipsy: my own younger daughter is named Barbara, though I know of no Romany followers.

Lawrence's book is, to speak with absolute freedom, an unfeeling and malicious assault upon me by a man who, if he had had any respect either for the conventions of civilised society, or for natural justice, would never have written it, and whose widow should in decency at least have waited until all the parties were dead before ever allowing it to be published. What makes it worse, however, is that the fiction is based wholly upon the untruths which Barbara (I am unashamed in such a cause to name names)

iv

must have told Lawrence about me, my mother and the rest of my family. The story kills the mother and crudely insults other family members. The Saywell wretch is however shewn forgiving his daughter when she subsequently behaves badly. In that respect, I fear that real life will deviate from the example set by fiction. I do not regret giving Barbara a name so easily associated with the barbarian and the barbarous, but I shall never again allow her under my roof. When I acquired my copy of the book she was apparently living with her mother in the south of France: in Aunt Jane's memorable words, 'in another country, remote and private, where, shut up together with little society, on one side no affection, on the other no judgment', it may reasonably be supposed that 'their tempers' will indeed become 'their mutual punishment'.

It was Barbara who was responsible for having the whole wretched business raked up again, and set out for the public to read: a business about which the public will, in its inimitable way, derisively speculate. I considered writing to Lawrence's widow threatening her with legal action if she did not desist from allowing the thing – undoubtedly[1] slimy, by the standards of the *Telegraph* obituary – to be printed. It first appeared in an ugly *de luxe* edition published in Italy, doubtless by the same pornographer who produced the *Chatterley* abomination, but the customary publications in Britain and the United States soon appeared. What held me back was simply the thought of receiving, back from her, her usual chaotic farrago of complaints about having to live off whatever her husband had failed to provide for her. Even pornography makes insufficient money for a grasping widow.

She has grown terribly stout, my other daughter Elsa told me a couple of years ago. I can truthfully say that I have no desire whatsoever to see her again: I prefer the woman I saw when she was, what, eighteen, straight as a ramrod, with a gaze as direct as

---

[1] I would have said 'unquestionably' if the word were not notoriously in use, philologically, in reference to the hazy recollections of amateur theories propounded in correspondence columns.

v

. . . I don't know what. It did for me, at any rate.

But hence this memoir. Lawrence may finally be under the sod, but is nevertheless responsible for a nasty piece of spite purporting to tell the truth about me and my marriage. One can only suppose that the man penned it so late in life that he did not have time to publish his unpleasantness himself (I do not forget an old story of his called 'Daughters of the Rector' or something similar which I am told also caricatured me and my daughters) .

So here I set out simply to recount the truth of the life and times of a man who – although fooled by one who turned out no better than a cheap pornographer – nevertheless lives to tell the tale: and tell it he will. I intend to set down the 'naked unblushing truth' of what happened; for, as Gibbon argued, such can be the 'sole recommendation of this personal narrative'. It is a rich enough subject: but it must also recount pain such as I never thought to experience, and would never wish on another human being.

ERNEST WEEKLEY.

NOTTINGHAM
29 September 1938.

CHAPTER I

I shall begin, in the best modern style, by observing myself. Seventy-four years old, admired and loved by students and friends, always tending to the ironical and the sarcastic, rarely (he confesses) at a loss for words, the happy possessor of a brain equipped with reference and quotation, drawn from a memory that as yet shows no sign of faltering; in huge demand, wherever English is spoken, for articles, for books, for wise words; perhaps happiest when in his study, but (he is regularly told) a marvellous natural communicator.

For I am, I believe, the first man of my generation to turn a strictly academic subject into a string of popular books without at any point compromising my academic standards. The plaudits have never stopped coming, even if my specialist colleagues have criticised my scholarly jocularity (I always remind them of Stevenson: 'Nothing like a little judicious levity'). But they are almost certainly jealous of my ability both to command an audience and to earn more than they can.

But I write this, at the age of seventy-four, in my Nottingham study, not in my Oxford or Cambridge College room, nor even in the University of London. Nottingham is a place without a University, only an imposing but slightly absurd University College. Did I nevertheless love it so much that I stayed on after growing famous, in spite of the host of flattering invitations to take up a prestigious University chair elsewhere? I did not. No such invitations ever came. Since 1913 I have been *persona non grata* in the University world. Nottingham decided against dismissing me, I believe, because it deemed me capable, like Kipping, of bringing it some renown, while remaining confident that I would never be able to leave (the title page of every one of my books loyally declares my position as 'Professor of French and Head of the Modern Language Department at University College, Nottingham', and I continue the tradition into my retirement). But I confess that, given a choice, I would rather I and my children could forget that the damned place (to set it in the vernacular) had ever existed. For the news splashed over the front page of the

PROOFS EW ARWW 5-6 Feb.1939

News of the World in October 1913, as my divorce was announced – 'To Live Her Own Life: Lady leaves husband and joins author' it ran (I still possess the cutting) – was quite enough to bring even my career to a standstill. *Le scandale du monde est ce qui fait l'offense*: I was never even promoted through the University hierarchy in Nottingham (there are many posts superior to that of Professor). The fact that my title pages also declare me 'Sometime scholar of Trinity College, Cambridge' indicates the nullification of the possibility of further promotion, while suggesting where, by rights, I might have found myself, even if – notoriously 'urban, squat, and packed with guile' – Cambridge people 'rarely smile', and would certainly not have enjoyed my books.

It is not incorrect to suggest that my life really started three times: once when I was born, once when I was thirty-three years old and met her, and once again the day she left me: but I do not contemplate the possibility of another start of that, or indeed of any other kind.

PROOFS EW ARWW 5-6 Feb.1939

CHAPTER II

I am conscious that such obviously self-pitying narratives as this need to be laced with material appealing to the vulgar imagination, to make them even moderately palatable. Let me start off, therefore, with sex: if only to demonstrate that pornographers have no special claim to truthful accounts of sexual experience. This will be territory not quite as new for me as it will be for the majority of my readers. I am proud to report that my *Etymological Dictionary*, unlike almost all dictionaries of the period, contains entries for both *clitoris* and *vulva*, the latter incidentally being defined as '*integument, cogn. with volvere, to turn*': i.e. something superficial, which turns away. As indeed she was, as indeed she did. Not many of my readers will spot that. Readers in the know may also enjoy the way I move from *adulterare* to the definition '*to commit adultery, corrupt*'.

But most of my readers will not have ventured on the perusal of such material: it is Lawrence who has been hailed the pioneer of sexually uninhibited writing. Let us see what we can do to match or even outdo him, without ourselves venturing into the slime.

Up to the age of thirty-four I had never experienced sexual indulgence with a woman. I was in fact almost ignorant sexually, except for undergoing the usual exploratory fumblings by the elder boys with the younger ones in a boys' school – provocations broken off, anyway, by my having to leave school when I was sixteen years old in order to earn for my family. I went to Training College for a year and started teaching at seventeen; my younger brother was still at the school where I taught. And I worked: my God I worked. But there is a sage maxim that schoolmastering is a very good profession – to get out of; and I got out of it just as soon as I could.

If however I am to make this a thoroughly accurate record, as I intend, I should add that I had not only worked but wanked: my God I wanked. Most nights of the week. I had read all I could of sex: the late Victorian sexual writing on which I managed to lay my hands had given me a fair idea of what to expect with a woman, and my imagination spilled over, appropriately, into the

ix

rest. Or so I thought. But it was also clear that my private world, the world peopled by my fertile imagination and by what I had gained by drawing on all the sexual writing and illustration I could discover, had really nothing to do with the world of actual people among whom I lived. My friends had sisters, my colleagues had wives; but they all seemed as out of bounds to me as me as the women of the street I inevitably encountered, on my way to and from the station. I was eternally polite, elegantly sarcastic, and ever so slightly flirtatious in female company; but the idea that I might make advances to one of the women I knew was utterly foreign to me. My parents hoped to see me settling down with a woman in marriage, but all that time during my 'teen' years, and my twenties, when I was working, qualifying myself, going from one University to another – supporting myself and doing my best to support a couple of my siblings too – the thought of marriage was perfectly impossible. I had not a penny to spare, except for what I spent on books: I lived hand to mouth, in rented property. I could no more propose marriage than I could fly. My private sexuality was all I could afford to indulge.

But one day – there she was. Out of the blue. The academic year 1896-7 I had spent in Freiburg, one of the most entirely enjoyable years of my life: working as a Professor of English, but living my life in German outside the classroom; I had lodgings upstairs at the *Deutscher Kaiser* in Güntersthalstraße, sharing the second floor with that cheerful reprobate Captain Otto Wagner. At Trinity I had gained a half blue, playing hockey for the University; but at the age of thirty-three, my athletic skills were mostly confined to billiards, where I was (I confess) a very fair player. I had been endowed by nature with a considerable reach, and legs longer than those of most people; I could reach across the table almost preternaturally (the name my colleagues conjured up for me that year was 'der langer Engländer'). And I could also think far ahead, allowing me to wipe the floor with my German opponent on more than one occasion. The bars of Freiburg were happily filled with billiard tables (there was one downstairs at the *Deutscher Kaiser*), and an English billiard player was something new for my German fellow-players. For my part I had to acquire a whole new language

x

for the game, things not translating as one might have expected. One does not, for example, find *die Tasche* but *das Loch* for the pocket: not *die Kanone* but (amazingly) *die Karambolage* for the cannon – and so on. I acquired this new vocabulary with relish and played all the better for the concentration it required, I suspect.

A colleague, near neighbour and regular fellow billiards player was my Head of Department, the English specialist Arnold Schröer; a man in his forties, an age which I especially appreciated, since up until then almost all my colleagues, wherever I had worked, had been ten or more years younger than me, the result of my having shouldered my way up through the educational system so late and so slowly (because I had had to hold down at least one and sometimes two jobs at the same time as working for my qualifications, working until I reeled). Schröer's flat, in the Turnseestraße, was only a couple of hundred yards from the *Deutscher Kaiser*; and it was he who introduced me to the delights of cigars, now a life-long passion (*Qui vit sans tabac n'est pas digne de vivre*).

And it was Schröer who – in the cold winter of my year in Freiburg – mentioned that, in the summer, we really should go and see these two ladies, the Blas sisters, who lived just a stroll away in Littenweiler, up on the Eichberg overlooking everything. They were old friends of his wife and the place was very beautiful, hillsides surrounded by fields and woods; and he really owed them a visit. They were in theory school-teachers – and yet their establishment (the *Höhere Mädchenpensionat Eichberghaus*), out on the edge of a village at that date, was not so much to teach superior young ladies as to *improve* them, to ensure they acquired the polish necessary for their acceptance in the wider world (meaning to fit them for the very best kinds of husbands). The sisters were, in consequence, surrounded by extraordinarily charming girls being readied for marriage – a real-life 'dream of fair women' – and I suspect that Schröer rather enjoyed his dutiful visits.

But these extraordinarily charming girls were also extraordinarily loud. The inside of the house, when we got there after a decent little walk the following June – it was certainly in

xi

the most beautiful situation, up a steep hill – was quite impossible, with waves of chattering and giggling resonating through it. We retreated to the garden up behind the house, away from the open windows so far as we could, for Kaffee und Kuchen. And there we made polite conversation (with a lot of respectful talk from the sisters about the gentility of the English), with just the occasional beautiful young lady crossing the grass near to us, parasol raised. Finally Schröer then took me round the estate, with its fields, its woods, its views down into the Dreisamtal and across to the hills the far side, and then we went up into the Eichberg wood. It was a lovely day, and it was a very lovely place.

Back in England later that year, having received what at the time I reckoned a flattering invitation to apply for the chair of modern languages at Nottingham University College, and having duly been appointed as its Professor of French (with duties running the German section as well), at last I had a full-time job. I looked forward to being able to save a little money, and do a little more of what I wanted. I started at Nottingham in January 1898; I acquired my first little property (of which I was vastly proud) and my first servant, in Nottingham Road, Basford; and by the summer I thought a holiday my due. I do not believe I had ever had a holiday before this one: and I was thirty-three years old. So I went back to Freiburg in the long vacation of 1898, to stay in my old lodgings at Karl Sütterlin's *Deutscher Kaiser*, and see the Schröers again, hoping to meet some others of my old friends; and I had another marvellous time.

A couple of days after I arrived I put the idea to Schröer that we might go back one afternoon to see the Blas sisters and their teeming, beautiful hordes, up at the *Eichberghaus*; and so we did, though – this time accompanied by Schröer's wife – we went by carriage. I must confess that my attitude towards charming young heiresses had undergone somewhat of a change since I had acquired an academic post and a salary which might have been reliable but was also astonishingly little. The thought of an aristocratic heiress falling in love with me, and changing my life for the better, was a fruitful fantasy which certainly helped me fall asleep the night before we set off for the Eichberg and the house

xii

on the hill.

The school holidays had just started, however, and the hosts of girl pupils were absent (one of the things, I learned, which had made the idea of a visit attractive to Frau Schröer). Just a few old friends of the family were staying and I found myself bowing my respects to Baron Friedrich von Richthofen and the Frau Baronin, who were, we learned, there with two of their daughters (neither of them visible). I could not click my heels in emulation of the Baron, but I was complimented upon my English gentlemanliness and – for an Englishman – my almost accent-free German, while we once again had our Kaffee und Kuchen; and then Schröer and I again went for a walk up through their gardens and sadly heiress-free fields and woods, leaving the women-folk and the Baron to chat.

But then, on our way back to pay our respects to the sisters, late in the afternoon, suddenly – there she was. I can find no other words, I am aware, in spite of having what I like to consider a considerable English vocabulary at my disposal. A girl in a meadow. I now know that, like me, she was simply visiting: she had been a pupil of the sisters once but was now staying at the *Eichberghaus* with her parents. I saw her first in a pink and white dress with a pink and white sunbonnet, from out of which her blond hair escaped . . . but she stood in the meadow and stared at me as if she could not take her eyes off me, with the most wonderful wide smile on her face. It was as if she knew me of old: I loved the feeling. Schröer had met her before and was able to effect introductions as necessary – her name was Frieda (I should say that this is the first time I have knowingly uttered or written down that name since 1913) – but I seemed to walk straight past any such thing as an introduction into knowing the girl for myself, as if I had already run my hand down her cheek and stroked her chin and turned her face towards me.

I did not, of course, do any of those things. But they seemed the most natural things in the world to do. Tennyson's words filled my mind: 'We needs must love the highest when we see it.'

I was also profoundly embarrassed, having developed the most overpowering and extraordinary erection while I stood looking at

PROOFS EW ARWW 5-6 Feb.1939

her, which I tried to conceal as best I could by holding my straw hat (doffed to meet her, naturally) absurdly down in front of me, as a kind of concealment. But it was what one might call a standing proof that I *wanted* her; wanted as I had never previously wanted any living being. It was at that moment that I discovered what wanting a woman meant, and how utterly important it was, in the whole scheme of things.

We strolled back down to the house together, with Schröer telling her that she ought to talk English with me, as I was an English Professor – and with her protesting that a Professor was the very last person with whom she would ever use her wretched school-English. We talked – in German – and while perfectly unacademic she struck me as extremely lucid about what she liked and what she did not. And though I watched her constantly, and never watched where I was going, somehow my feet surmounted every obstacle, eventually every step and stair-case, without my noticing. I was in a kind of trance, brilliantly observant, totally focussed, entirely locked within my new awareness of this marvellous young creature. She was not very tall but full-breasted and clearly very active, as she hopped and jumped her way down the hillside towards the house, with a long nose (just a little tilted towards the tip) and a very determined little round chin – and with that fantastically wide mouth, which defined the whole wonderfully steady and appealing character of her face.

We did not stay long with the sisters and their guests; but just long enough for us to agree that we must certainly all meet again later in the week, and which day it should be; and so back to Freiburg, with my erection at last subsiding.

She, I later learned, was as struck with me as I was with her. But now, even to myself I cannot really convey the impact on me, the desire for her which she instigated and which possessed me completely. I wanted her and had to see her again. That face, that mouth, that nimble, full-breasted body, that sense of a cat smiling in the sunshine and finding it good. I thought about nothing else, even when I was doing something else. I was also buoyed up with what felt like inexhaustible energy.

How did it all start, then? Because I fell devastatingly in love –

PROOFS EW ARWW 5-6 Feb.1939

and lust – for the first time in my life. She responded to my subsequent declarations of love with amazement and, I fear, something like compassion for my age. I don't *think* she confused me with her father as a person to love (though, with her, almost anything is possible). But she was also, I know, like the rest of her family (Else apart) hugely impressed with my title of Professor; she looked up to me at once, perhaps enjoyed the thought of my excellent professorial salary (an untruth, unfortunately: Nottingham paid terribly little), certainly observed my still excellent figure, liked my moustaches (and perhaps imagined for a moment what they might be like when in intimate contact with herself) and probably thought of me as potentially her husband before Schröer had even finished introducing us to each other. I cannot say how much further in the direction of sensual satisfaction her imagination might have taken her, at such a moment: her imagination was capable of almost anything, as I would sadly find out. All I knew was that I could not help imagining what she would look like without her clothes on: I could strip her naked in my imagination, in an instant.

But that's enough about how it all started. My courtship, my marriage, and my subsequent experiences as a married man I will describe later. The great questions – for me and for you, doubtless, lured into reading this – remain 'when and how did such a wonderful beginning go wrong?' The answer to the first question, according to our most recent psychoanalysts, would be 'the day I was born in 1865, in love with my mother'; the answer to the other question is, most certainly, 'because I was fooled'.

CHAPTER III

As a child, I had the huge advantage of growing up in a bookish home and with a bookish father. This however has to be weighed against the considerable disadvantage of being brought up in a home where there was never enough money. I was originally a second son, and then at the age of fifteen, when my poor elder brother Montague suffered his dreadful end, I became the eldest son, having acquired (by then) seven further siblings, for whom I inevitably felt in some degree responsible; my father's work as Relieving Officer for the Hampstead workhouse was very badly paid, and we children almost overflowed our cramped little rented house.

But, having learned my letters earlier than most children, at the age of five or six I had started to read omnivorously while also developing an insatiable curiosity about words. My father was ready to enlighten me when I was puzzled as to the relation between disease and decease, though that between idolatry and adultery must have caused him some embarrassment. But one of my favourite books, found when I was a child of eight, was a dictionary of synonyms. I was entranced with my discovery that some words meant almost the same thing as others, though with slight differences which could change everything; so that 'abject' could easily mean 'wretched', but that 'wretched' could also shade into 'servile', from which it was only a step to what I learned was the culminating word 'despicable'. The words, so set down, were in themselves descending steps; meaning that one must always hold one's head up, one must never be seen as abject, or one might be condemned to this terrible downward progress, to which the dictionary had opened my eyes. That was just one example among many; and such things stayed with me, in my extremely (that is, rather: one must not exaggerate) retentive memory.

Odd, this, for an eight year old, you may think. It gets worse. By the age of nine, I was soaked in the novels of the great Sir Walter Scott, whose picturesque, too often sham-antique, vocabulary had helped make me a word hunter in the first place. But then, when I

PROOFS EW ARWW 5-6 Feb.1939

was eleven, came this marvellous opportunity. My great uncle Boulden had inherited rather a good boys' school, Dane Hill House, down in Kent, and he offered my father the chance of sending three of his boys to it, without fees; just the customary costs of clothes and books. It seemed obvious that Montague (then fourteen), I (eleven) and Bruce (nine) would be the three, as the ones who had shewn by far the most promise (Charles was never a scholar, as he cheerfully admitted). Accordingly we were placed at the school that same autumn. I can honestly say that I was the one who benefited most; the row of prizes I won testifies to that. History, English, Geography, Mathematics – I carried them all off, not just once but year after year, for six years. And it was at school that I discovered Tennyson, who stays with me as the best poet of all.

But when I was fifteen came the awfulness of Montague's death. At the time I knew rather little about what had happened but my brother Bruce was closer to his elder brother and had learned a good deal. At the start of his last year at the school – he was a promising mathematician – poor Monty had fallen desperately in love with the daughter of the school caretaker and had, I suspect, from what could later be learned, actually embarked on carnal relations with her (Bruce knew nothing about this, at least). Her father had however discovered what was going on, and had threatened to expose Montague to the school authorities if he did not hand over a series of increasingly large sums of money. Montague, I knew, was an extremely moral individual, and would certainly have wanted to marry any girl he had had such relations with, though marriage with this individual would to most people have been out of the question. But her father's threats were a form of especially horrible duress. In this situation – and also wrongly believing, from something the father had said – that the girl had turned against him – one miserable January day he went out in the fields backing on to the school grounds and hanged himself from a tree. His absence was quickly noticed, and he was searched for, but it was not for several days that his body was discovered.

My parents never learned the truth, fortunately; his death was reported to them as being the result of an accident in which he fell

xvii

from the tree where he was found, his body being discovered only later. And the story never got into the newspapers, either, thanks to the astuteness of our Headmaster, the Rev. Charles Boulden. The caretaker was warned that if he said anything, action would be started against him for extorting money by menaces, and that he faced a term in prison if found guilty – which he certainly would be (some of his threatening notes and demands had been found among Montague's things). The caretaker was immediately dismissed from his post, and the Headmaster obliged him to leave Margate. The girl, fortunately, was not pregnant, and vanished with her father.

And so it was that I became my parents' eldest son, and took on the responsibilities accruing; and I left school at the end of the summer term the following year, in order to train as a teacher (it being obvious that I was academically gifted) and to earn not only my own living but to assist my father in bringing up the younger children. I went to Finsbury Training College, obtained my Teaching Certificate, and after a brief experience as a teacher in Colchester I came back to work at Dane Hill School, where my brother Bruce still was. What I earned then enabled him to stay at the school until he was eighteen; after a brief period in the bank (to earn his keep) he started to study for the ministry, as he had always intended.

I do not incidentally know from where Bruce managed to get his belief in God. Not from the Weekleys, for sure: we were a Godless lot. But the Bouldens were religious, and their predilections may have run through the McCowans and so into my mother and my brother. I respect the Church of England as an institution which encourages moral behaviour and a belief in hierarchy, and which employs on a daily basis some of the finest prose and verse ever produced in Britain; to be honest, though, I draw the line at Christianity. I would later enjoy a couple of quiet little thrusts in my *Etymological Dictionary*, where for example my quotation for *Christadelphian* (from 'Christ' and 'brother') mentioned the 1918 event in which a certificate of exemption was issued to one of that sect who had been fined for knocking a horse's eye out, while a mention of the *Thundering Legion* referred to 'a militarily

xviii

convenient thunder-storm brought on by the prayers of its Christian members'. But having a brother who is a cleric at times comes in handy; Bruce was able to officiate at my marriage to Frieda in the brand-new English Church in Freiburg-Wiehre.

I will however add that I intend to leave my family out of this narrative for the most part (a few events in 1912 will be an exception). They have already suffered more than enough from Lawrence's travesty.

It is incidentally easy to see how my thinking about matters entirely distinct is here so naturally channelled back into thinking about *her*, without any obvious provocation. She remains simply *there*, inexplicably *there*, in my life, even after all this time.

PROOFS EW ARWW 5-6 Feb.1939

CHAPTER IV

But back to 1883. I cannot now conceive of how hard I was working at this point of my career. Not only was I starting as a teacher, having barely qualified; a year later, at the age of nineteen, I started to study for a London University external B.A. degree, having to teach myself everything, including how to sit examinations! This first degree took me four years; and, with it, I was be able to get employment at William Briggs's University Correspondence College in 1887, and would also eventually be able to move up to Cambridge (a spiritual home, if ever I had one). But for the moment it meant that – with a little money borrowed from my mother – I was able to go abroad for a year, to a foreign University, which I reckoned the only way to get deeply acquainted with a language. Bern/Berne was good for both French and German; and I worked as a tutor there, to support myself. Then back to England, where my job with William Briggs was secure, for full-time teaching and duties at the Correspondence College in London: four years of that, setting examinations and marking them too. This was when I met (as another student and teacher) H. G. Wells, an energetic slip of a man full of bright ideas. But going into the academic world was not his goal – while it had become mine. Looking back I can barely understand how I did it, but during those years with Briggs I also did a deal of academic work, so that I was awarded a Masters Degree in French and German in 1892. Only then could I do what I had always wanted to do – try to study at Cambridge: and Briggs offered me a job in Cambridge too, so that I could go on preparing French language books to be sold to schools and colleges. I went up to Trinity in 1893; and in my second year I was awarded a Major Scholarship, the first ever given for foreign languages. I had a wonderful time; I played hockey for the University a couple of times (another use for those long arms), and got my half-blue, I took Trinity's Vidil prize for French, and in 1896 I got a first in the Tripos with special distinctions in French and German, the first time that had ever been done. I had gone on working for Briggs in my spare moments; and here I found that I had a real talent for the kind of

xx

work involved in setting up the kind of books which he (and his publishing friend Clive) wanted. And I earned a penny or two as well, which allowed me, after Cambridge, to go abroad for another year, this time to the Sorbonne in Paris, studying Romance philology under Gaston Paris and Antoine Thomas. This study, combined with my Cambridge degree, qualified me to go abroad yet again, to the University of Freiburg, for a whole year – and this time as a full-time lecturer (in English), for the best year of my life. Then a few weeks in Paris, polishing up my accent after a year of German in Freiburg, before coming back to Cambridge (a kind of economic home to me, it had also become) for three months' slog with the examinations and books for Briggs – and then the luck (as I thought it, at the time) of being selected for that post by Nottingham.

It is easy to write all this down now. It was not so easy at the time. But the non-stop pressure of work was something to which I had become accustomed. My 'holiday' in the summer of 1898 (even now I instinctively put it in inverted commas, it remains such a novelty) was something very special indeed.

And I have already described how special it became . . . because of the girl in the meadow. I was invited back to the *Eichberghaus* for Kaffee und Kuchen later in the week after meeting her; and on this occasion, during a long family session, I was able really to talk to her; but what mattered was that I was *with* her, not that we talked. I cannot now imagine what on earth we talked about.

And then the idea of a stroll was put forward; and Schröer and his wife and Frieda and I and her younger sister Johanna (at that date, rather thin and gawky, though very striking) set off up the hill again . . . I fancy that the shrewd Frau Schröer knew very well what was happening, because she made no attempt to interrupt the heart-to-heart which Frieda and I were sharing, but set herself to distracting her husband, who would otherwise certainly have been constantly coming over to me with all kinds of linguistic insights. That walk in the evening sun, 'All in the blue unclouded weather', remains to me one of the magical times of my life, though again I cannot now recall a word of what we said. We were simply so close, so understanding, so intimate, so quickly. My mutinous

xxi

erection manifested itself again, but I had taken the precaution (although it was a warm day) of wearing a thicker pair of trousers; I had only the one jacket with me, my old homespun herring-bone. But my erection remained as a constant proof of what I felt, and what I wanted.

We got back, and were polite together with the von Richthofens (her father felt very stiff, still, though friendly; her mother struck me as profoundly sensible). But before we finally left, going back into the house, Frieda and I managed somehow to put ourselves at the back of the queue of people, and as we passed another doorway, Frieda grabbed my hand and gently tugged me after her, and I found myself chest to chest with her (what a chest, I should remark in passing), and we were very gently kissing each other before either of us really knew what was happening.

At least, before I knew. To be honest, what happened was that she kissed me and I managed some kind of flustered response. She was a great deal more experienced, when it came to flirtation, than I was; she had had more than one officer boy-friend before (there had been a von Richthofen cousin, way back, and there actually still was one, called Kurt von something, who was in fact my direct rival, though I never knew it at the time: she told me about him years later). But there had never been anything more than kissing, in these earlier flirtations of hers, she insisted. I however had never even had the kissing; and it was quite extraordinary to feel those lips of hers so soft, so astonishingly soft ; I wondered if she were aware of my erection, up against her as it was at that moment, and what she would make of it if she were (perhaps she would just think that my cigar case had slipped into an odd position). It took only a moment, however, and then we were dashing after the rest of the party to catch them up before we all got to the front door, and were encountering maid-servants with hats and sticks.

But we had eyes only for each other; and that kiss had been extraordinary. Again I saw Frau Schröer doing her best for me, talking animatedly to the von Richthofen parents, giving Frieda and me a chance to shake hands and hold hands for a moment, without its being noticed. And then we were gone.

xxii

CHAPTER V

In the carriage on the way home, Frau Schröer took her chance of having just a word with me, to say that she could not help seeing how impressed I was with Frieda, and what a tremendously handsome girl Frieda certainly was, to be sure; and I took my chance, in a way quite new for me, feeling as I was thoroughly 'up to snuff', of saying how beautiful I thought Frieda was, too . . . and Frau Schröer then said that she had actually invited the von Richthofens to dinner the following day, and that she hoped I would enjoy the occasion. I smiled at her and she smiled happily at me before her husband leaned across to ask about the proper German translation of the English architectural word *bolection* (goodness knows where he had found that: reading about Fonthill, perhaps). I had no idea.

So what happened next? A day spent up at the University talking with Schröer about words (but, I must admit, having to force myself to attend, though I suspect I smiled a good deal) until, finally, dinner in the Schröers' flat . . . and I was seated next to Frieda (the youngest daughter Johanna was fortunately not present). The Schröers encouraged me to talk about myself to the von Richthofen parents (and thus to Frieda), so I told them about my life from my school-days onwards – and that turned out to impress her deeply, the work I had done, the years I had spent supporting my family, the way I had had dinner with my parents in 1894 and told them afterwards that they had just had dinner with a scholar of Trinity (it was the week when I got news of my scholarship). She watched me, she attended to me, she asked intelligent questions; she seemed to go out of her way to understand me and to sympathise with me.

I later learned that she was in particular struck not by the unremitting hard work but by the fact that my family and I were so solidly grounded in work and mutual trust and reliance; she inevitably compared us with her own parents' constant quarrels, her father's gambling, the awful uncertainty of everyday life in Metz – things of which, of course, I had no idea. But my life and my parents' life seemed to her so calm, so stable, so directed and

xxiii

certain, by contrast. I saw Frau von Richthofen sending some piercing glances in my direction, but the Baron himself appeared far more interested in the boar's trotters we had for Vorspeise, and the venison for the main course, after the fish, than he was in anything which I had to say. I was later to discover that he had once issued his three daughters with the instruction that they were at liberty to marry anyone they chose, with three exceptions: a Jew, a gambler, and an Englishman. And the eldest (Else: I shall come to her in a bit) would marry Edgar Jaffe, economist and Jew: the youngest (Johanna) would marry Max von Schreibershofen, general staff officer and gambler; and Frieda married me. And all three marriages came to grief. Perhaps the old man had more sense than I allowed him.

But what I was feeling, that July day in 1898, was that – though all good things come to an end – this one was *not* going to come to an end. Although I had only a fortnight left (I was due to leave for Bern for more meetings with old colleagues), by the end of the meal at the Schröers I felt more convinced than ever that I not only wanted to kiss this adorable girl again, but that I also intended to spend the rest of my life repeating the experience. What other, better basis for a marriage would I ever find? Before I left Freiburg, I would have to find out a way of communicating this to her.

Readers in these inhibition-free late 1930s will not appreciate how, in our Victorian 1880s and 1890s, we had to rely on extraordinarily little personal information in forming the conclusions which led us into engagement and marriage; and how, even then, actually communicating with a person was fraught with difficulty. Seeing each other alone was not, in the middle- and upper-classes, something that happened until formal parental permission had been given; nor was the writing of letters usually allowed (though it often happened). When a chance like sitting next to each other came, we had to be preternaturally attuned to the concentration evinced by a lifted eyebrow, a gaze held for longer than usual, an expressive sigh, in extreme cases the holding of a hand or (in my case) the momentary kiss. Only those signs told us what was happening in the other person: told us this was

xxiv

or was not the person with whom we wished to spend our lives. And not surprisingly we sometimes – we regularly – got it wrong. That was a Thursday. The following morning, at their flat, where I had gone to look at some of Schröer's papers, Frau Schröer took me on one side and said she could not help observing how well I was getting on with Frieda, and – she did not wish to intrude on my privacy, but she knew something of the problem of being from another culture and being accustomed to other forms of etiquette – would I like her perhaps to say something to Frieda's parents, with the aim of allowing me to go on visiting her and seeing her during the few days which I had left? Frieda herself would also be leaving Freiburg soon. I said I would very much like that; but I would actually like to ask her father for permission myself – and that I was profoundly impressed with Frieda, and had started to think of asking her father if we might get engaged . . . after a pause, of course, during which we would get to know each other better. Frau Schröer smiled at this, and suggested that an engagement might be a *little* too hasty; but that we could both go to the Eichberg later that day, if I would like that, and I could have a word with the parents while she had a word with Frieda; that would be perhaps the best way to handle the matter. I was hugely grateful to her for guiding me through the etiquette of such a relationship – all the language-learning in the world, however well conducted by the best teachers at the best universities, does not educate one into the ways in which relationships are furthered, and engagements proceeded with, in the superior ranks of society – but I later learned that Frau Schröer too came from a Baronial family, had spent two years at the *Eichberghaus* as a pupil, and knew all the ways to proceed when it came to the polite forwarding of desire for a girl under the roof of the Blas sisters.

So, up at the *Eichberghaus*, I dutifully talked to the Baron about his daughter, saying what a privilege it would be for me to get to know her better, she being the descendent (I wanted to say 'scion' but was not sure of the German for that honourable word[2]) of such

---

[2] I know now: der Schößling (Grillparzer writes of 'die Schößlinge der gefällten Königseiche').

a well known and highly-thought-of aristocratic family. In the meanwhile, Frau Schröer went and told Frieda (I learned later) that I was not only asking parental permission to get to know her, but that she (Frau Schröer) was privately sure I wanted to get engaged – meaning that I loved her and wanted to marry her. And that it of course depended on Frieda herself whether anything were to come of it all.

We had fortunately arrived around the middle of that long pause between lunch and tea, so were not this time troubled by the Baron's attention being focussed elsewhere (it now seems to me probable that Frau Schröer had been intelligent, too, about the timing of our arrival). When I began to talk with him, he turned out to be more than friendly. The title of Professor, indeed, seemed to matter even more to him than it had done to Frieda; he deferred to me as a super-intellectual being who would very rarely have any dealings with lesser mortals or lesser things. He treated me as a very rare bird indeed, flying in superlatively rarefied air, but one he would be happy to see flying into his own aviary. He did not seem to have taken much notice of the things I had been saying about my family's poverty, or its class status, and I was in no hurry to remind him.

What Frau von Richthofen suggested, however, when we eventually told her of how matters stood, was that although Frieda and I might wish, when we knew each other a little better, to consider ourselves informally engaged, she would only be happy for a formal engagement (or indeed a marriage) to go ahead when Frieda and she had had the chance to visit England to meet my parents, and when Frieda had got to know a little of England too. (Events showed that she did not actually mean this: she meant, when she and the Baron had had a chance to get to know me better.) That would only be fair to a girl such as Frieda, who had (her mother insisted) so very little experience of the world. I refrained from pointing out that, as there were already two men in Berlin hoping to marry her, she clearly must have *some* experience to go on. They must have kissed her – probably passionately – and I could not have offered up the name of a single girl I had even kissed.

xxvi

But I immediately agreed to the Frau Baronin's suggestion, saying that it seemed both profoundly sensitive and sensible, though it left me unhappily conscious that it ensured that I would get no further than kissing this immensely desirable girl for another six months or so. (In fact it was twelve months.) What I barely considered was that the Frau Baronin was in reality very unsure about her daughter getting engaged to – or even worse marrying – a man from such a very lower-middle-class family as my own; my description of my work as a young man, which I had thought so impressive to everyone around the Schröers' dinner table, had succeeded in conveying only too well my family's poverty and our class status (the very lowest rung possible of the middle class). And I had aunts who actually kept a shop! The Frau Baronin had taken all this in, beady-eyed and stony-faced, and had *not* been impressed.

The Baron himself was also unimpressed, but I eventually discovered that it was not my intellectual status which mattered so overwhelmingly to him, in counterbalancing my class status, but my income. Getting an expensive daughter off his hands seemed his main, even his only, aim.

My class-status, it turned out, was also one of Frieda's concerns, but she turned my wanting to get engaged to her into an opportunity for a daring and rebellious act: an upper-crust girl like her letting herself be carried off by a peasant like me! She positively enjoyed what she saw as the class discrepancy. I confess I found it all just a nuisance.

But all that came to matter only later. Before we left the *Eichberghaus* that afternoon, I had had – in the discreet company of Frau Schröer – a chance to speak privately to Frieda, and to arrange with her to come out on to the Eichberg itself the following day at 11.00, to meet (we agreed to meet at the spring half-way up the hill, in the woods, which we had passed when walking that way two days earlier).

That evening, back at the Schröers flat, Arnold was full of admiration at the speedy way in which I had proceeded, though he mourned the fact that for the rest of my time in Freiburg my attention would doubtless be focussed on this girl, and not on his great enterprise of the dictionary, for which he still so much needed my help. I said I thought I was capable of carrying both my assistance, and my love for Frieda, through to triumphantly successful conclusions – or some such thing; but for the first time in my life's history, something of equal importance to linguistic studies had come home to me.

CHAPTER VI

The following day – this was the Friday – I refused the Schröers' offer of the carriage to take me down to the Eichberg; I set off on foot, promising myself a pleasant stroll before getting to the fountain at about eleven. I got there, with typical Weekley punctuality, at about five minutes before the hour, but remained in the shade of the trees, just a few yards away from the fountain itself, smoking a thoughtful cigarette while trying to calm the excitement which possessed me. I had never felt anything like it: but never before had I waited for the arrival of the girl I loved.

Frieda was late, as I later learned she habitually was. In this case she had not remembered the way to the fountain, and had had to track down a woodsman who knew where it was; it was getting towards half-past-eleven before she appeared in the company of a brawny one-armed man with an axe, whom she had commandeered to find the way. The man, fortunately, turned and left with a gesture of the hand which suggested a military salute – he probably *was* an ex-soldier, it now occurs to me – and Frieda came across the grass towards me. She was out of breath, panting and perspiring, and her chest was rising and falling. None of this made her any the less attractive, I must say. She was so *bright* in the sun. This time I took the lead in kissing her, though on the cheek, not the mouth, really no more than as a greeting – and then we simply strolled together and talked about the squirrels and the trees and the marvellous views and the Blas sisters and her sisters and her upbringing and everything in the world . . . it was a kind of long getting to know one another. It only came to an end when she suddenly said 'I was due back for lunch at two: what time is it?' It was a quarter to three; we hurried together, hand-in-hand some of the way, back down to the house. This was rather embarrassing; most lunch things had already been cleared away, and the Baron and Baronin were nowhere to be seen. But Fräulein Julie Blas was there: and she was smiling in a most knowing way, while telling me that the kitchen would be very happy to make up a cold collation, in place of the lunch I had missed. I expressed my gratitude, and was soon sitting down with Frieda out of doors, with

xxix

good things on the table before us. So many things were now the first: this was actually our first meal alone together.

Afterwards, Frieda yawned and stretched herself (an action I found astonishingly alluring, it was so suggestive) and said that it was her habit, as it was of her whole family, to lie down for twenty minutes after luncheon. I very much wanted to say that it was just the kind of thing I also enjoyed, and that I would be happy to accompany her; but of course I said no such thing. I said I would just stroll in the garden, and would see her in half an hour or so.

And so that was what happened; and over the next few days I found myself playing my new rôle in the family, accepted as a kind of honorary son; sitting with the Baron over coffee while happily expressing my ignorance of hunting, and hearing all about it; sitting with the Frau Baronin, hearing all about Frieda as a child; sitting and playing cards with Frieda, and then walking with her, every day more in love with her. It was a marvellous time; it felt exactly right that, the following Saturday, a radiant August day, I should have had the extraordinary privilege of lunching with the great Sir James Murray (first and chief editor of the *New English Dictionary*) and Professor Friedrich Kluge, my sometime chief and teacher at Freiburg, not only a great lexicographer but the most learned and most beloved of 'Germanists'; and that Frieda should have been there too. I should record that Murray refused to drink the delicious Riesling provided by his hosts, but insisted on water, a fluid which at a German University in those days was thought to have been created entirely for the use of the lower animals. But he also invited me – and my fiancée, as I ventured to put it – to Oxford .

The rest of the time I spent over in Littenweiler . . . and this happy state went on for the rest of my time, with my being heartily invited to visit them in Metz, and my promising to do so after my long-arranged visit to Bern.

And so came the Monday before I was due to leave (I was departing very early on the Tuesday). I went to see the Baron mid-afternoon and said that I would, after all, like to ask him to approve my formal engagement with Frieda, without waiting until she had been to visit England; that I would however want her to visit

xxx

England before she married me, and an ideal time would be in December; I would come to Metz, and then travel with Frieda (together with him, or her mother, or one of her sisters) to England for her to meet my parents and see a little of the country. (This plan I had worked out with Frieda beforehand.) He looked perfectly prepared for this development, but said he would have to consult with Frieda's mother, and vanished for half an hour. Fräulein Julie Blas found me sitting by myself and took care of me by telling me the history of the house, and of her work there (she seemed to remember every pupil for the past forty years, including Frau Schröer) . . . till the Baron came back, together with the Frau Baronin. They told me that they approved of my plan; that I could announce my formal engagement to Frieda; and that I should not only come and see them briefly in Metz, after my Bern visit, but that I should come to Metz in December and stay some days; and that Frieda and her mother would then travel across to England with me, and an introduction both to my parents and to England could take place. I did not yet dare suggest that Frieda and I should be married in the spring; enough had been gained for one afternoon.

I wanted to go and see Frieda at once to tell her the news but it turned out that she had already been hard at work persuading her mother to accept the new plan, and as soon as the arrangements were concluded, she was invited in. We exchanged a polite, chaste kiss; and then I produced the engagement ring which Frieda and I had chosen together on the Saturday afternoon, when we had strolled back to Littenweiler. It was not very grand, but – after an appropriate display of astonishment – it was appropriately admired by Frieda's parents. I was due back with the Schröers for the evening, so at this point thanked both parents as elegantly as I could, shook hands with the Baron, shook hands with the Frau Baronin (I was not sure if kissing on both cheeks was expected, but clearly it was not: I would subsequently learn the etiquette from Frau Schröer) . . . and was permitted to make my way to the house door with Frieda, and so out and down the drive. We held hands very tightly and she pressed herself to me most seductively until, at the gate, we kissed long and (for the first time) deeply too,

xxxi

not just once but twice. But then I had to go, with promises to keep and making many promises too. And so I went to Bern, which was now not as enjoyable as I had hoped: I was too eager to leave again, and travel back to Metz.

In Metz they put me up in a strictly Protestant hotel, the *Deutscher Hof*, just a short tram-ride from their house in Montigny; and there it was arranged I would stay again, when I came over to visit them in the winter vacation.

And so I travelled back to England, with an embroidered heart-shaped cushion from Frieda in my possession, to keep me lovingly reminded of her and her unchanging heart, she insisted. I must say that I still find all this extraordinarily touching, although I am conscious of the most terrible irony in it, too. But I want to describe it as it was. It was love, quite simply.

PROOFS EW ARWW 5-6 Feb.1939

CHAPTER VII

The autumn passed in a busier than ever whirl of exam preparations, book writing, proof correcting, teaching, working for the UCC, running my Department, and writing long letters to Frieda. Her letters were also long; and though she occasionally dropped into English, I realised that her sense of inadequacy about her 'school English' was indeed well founded.

A word about language, before I go any further. German was our language of communication, now and for a very long time: not until the children were all born and growing up did we sometimes find ourselves conversing in English – and that mostly because a third person, an English friend for example, was present. The children grew up speaking German; but both Frieda and I were confident that, as soon as they were with children of their own age, they would quickly learn all the English they needed, and this is exactly what happened. By the time they were seven or eight years old, they were to all intents and purposes what philologists have learned to call bi-lingual, speaking two languages with perfect ease and freedom. At home, they were always addressed in German by their mother and their nurse; to balance things out, I took to speaking to them in English. Without noticing what they were doing, they adapted their own language accordingly, exactly as I had hoped they would.

But although Frieda learned good English in the long run, she always retained an astonishingly German (to be exact, Metzisch) accent, and her 'th' pronunciation was never good. Her writing revealed at once the faults of her education, but I resolved never to correct her German, only her English. Nevertheless, I was often impressed by the directness and naturalness of her writing. Letters to my parents and to hers during the autumn of 1898 had, meanwhile, to settle the matter of when we would meet in December, and how we would travel. We resolved that it would be the Frau Baronin's turn to go into an hotel in Dover while Frieda and I would travel in the company of my parents up to Hampstead (her mother was insistent that she would play no further part after delivering Frieda safely into the hands of her future parents-in-law: she wanted Frieda to go it alone, to see how it would be). We had originally thought that a family party of Weekleys, along with Frieda, would then go up to Nottingham, but that seemed to be an unnecessary complication – with the problem of where we should all stay when we got there. Frieda was sad not to see the house in Nottingham whose mistress she would become, but I procured a photograph for her, at least. As the dates could be made to coincide, we agreed that Frieda and I would celebrate Christmas with my parents in Hampstead; and then I would take Frieda back down to Dover, where she and her mother would travel back by boat and train to Metz for Silvester. The only odd thing seemed to be the way we would be leaving the Frau Baronin all alone in a hotel in Dover over Christmas, but she insisted that she would not mind in the least; if anything, the prospect of being away from Metz (and away from the Baron) for nine or ten days seemed a cause of happiness, not the reverse.

Anyway, it all worked out very well. It took me almost exactly twenty-four hours to get to Metz from London (I left Nottingham by the nine a.m. train, and was in Metz by half past two the following afternoon). For the first time I met Frieda's rather formidable elder sister Else. Everyone had supposed that because we were both University people (first as students, then as teachers), we would automatically get on. Just the opposite. Else had no very high opinion of Nottingham as a University College (she was at Heidelberg) and clearly blamed my unusual route to University teaching as the reason for my being stuck in an unenviable hole with no immediate prospect of release. She was clearly critical of the fact that I was not working for a doctorate, and never had done, and also expressed so strongly her sense of the world as a place needing reform and change that I grew sure that some of her passion was aimed at me – for working away in my own small corner, at my own small concerns, and not doing anything to make the world better. We parted amicably enough, but it was the amicability of people who know they would certainly oppose each other if push came to shove. The fact that I seemed determined to look after Frieda was almost the only thing about me of which Else seemed to approve.

xxxiv

I then had to organise travel for a very determined lady of fifty and an exceptionally skittish school-girl. They had bought their own railway tickets but almost everything that cost money on the journey I had to provide: steamer tickets, lunch and breakfast, for example. And when we finally got to England on the steamer around two in the afternoon, my parents were waiting on the quay for us; and, as usual, my mother was sublimely unconscious of there being anything odd about Frieda and her mother not being able to speak or understand English, or not understanding her immediately while she rattled away. Frieda did her very best with what English she had, but the Baronin remained a little frosty. It was honestly with some relief that we left her in Dover and travelled on with my parents. However, my mother accepted Frieda as my fiancée very lovingly. My father was more restrained, as always, though I could see how much he admired her, but when we got to Hampstead, Maude did her very best to be welcoming, and even George overcame his tendency to be lugubrious and joined in the fun.

But even that word 'fun' reminds me of how aloof the Frau Baronin had remained; and it was all a trifle disappointing for Frieda and me. Even on our journey back down to Dover together, after a week in Hampstead, although I had suggested to my mother that it was really not necessary for Frieda and me to be chaperoned all the way, all the time, my mother held firm to the agreements previously made and sent Maude with us, to keep us in order. As a result, Frieda and I had only had a few mornings alone together, when we walked on Hampstead Heath in spite of the wind and rain; there was literally nowhere we could go in Well Walk, as the house was heaving with the family over the holidays. Down in Dover, Frieda would be catching the evening boat-train with her mother, but Maude and I said goodbye mid-afternoon for our own return journey to London. And that was that; Frieda and I kissed decorously as we parted, under the stern gaze of her mother and my sister, and promised each other to write and to say how much we loved each other. But one could hardly say that our relationship had in any way been advanced by this visit. The best thing that had happened was that Frieda had found my parents enormously loving.

On the train journey back to London, Maude was inquisitive almost to a fault; *how* did I know that this young girl would be a good wife, *how* did I know she would be able to organise a household properly, *how* could I be sure that with her limited English she would not be cheated by every tradesman in Nottingham? All I could do was swear that she was an intelligent girl, quick to learn, and with a sensible head on her shoulders, and would no more get cheated in England than she was in Germany (though as I swore this I was very conscious that Frieda seemed to know nothing at all about the running of the German household, the latter being entirely in the hands of her mother and the cook).

It was possible for me to get away for a week at Easter, and spend it in Metz; and it had become clear that the wedding would have to be in the summer (and for reasons of summer holidays, August was the chosen month). Both Frieda and I very much liked the idea of getting married in Freiburg, where we had fallen in love, and of which she had so many happy memories; and the fact that there was – just round the corner from the Schröers – a brand-new English church, ready for us to get married in it, settled the matter. My brother Bruce was booked for the occasion (and would have to come to Germany for the first time). The Easter visit would only be fleeting, unfortunately, but half a loaf was better than no bread, and we took our chance of at last spending some time together; and if anything I was more head over heels in love with her after those five days together than I had ever been before.

If I were to attempt to sum up my feelings for her at this stage – to say what I had learned about her so far – it would however be astonishingly little. I knew she was abundantly attractive, I felt certain she was attracted to me. But what she was *like*, I could not have told you. All I could have offered would have been words like 'tender' and 'sweet' and 'lively'. I might have ventured 'knowing what she wants' – but I can now see how totally subjective all these attributes are; they are entirely what I, in my own mind, chose to perceive in her. They have nothing to do with the person she was, with that extraordinary combination of aristocratic self-possession and simple, unapologetic sensuality which I got to know when we were married. She knew what she wanted, and how to get it: and she almost always got it. I have reason to believe that I was the first man with whom she slept, but if the opportunity of having another man had (somehow) come her way during the months of our engagement, I now have no hesitation in declaring that she would have taken it: and still have happily married me in the summer of 1899.

Her religion seemed to me typically continental. She wanted to go to church at Easter and at Christmas, and there – the von Richthofens were Protestant but the Marquiers Catholic – she genuflected and crossed herself; but that apart I saw no trace in her of any kind of belief: in God, or indeed in anything. She turned out to have absolutely no care for or interest in morals as they are normally understood; she had no patience with idealism or indeed with any kind of ethical system. But I really had no idea of any of this until much later on. It was the merest chance that, up to this point, I should have been with her only at Christmas and Easter, and have seen her appropriately pious.

PROOFS EW ARWW 5-6 Feb.1939

CHAPTER VIII

The wedding would be in Freiburg, but the arrangements around that were complex and, I quickly found, not handled well by the parents of the bride – in Germany, as in England, the bride's family are perforce in charge. I had planned to write a whole chapter here about our engagement and about the wedding but find that I have almost nothing to say. I had taken care to obtain a term's leave of absence (unpaid), to cover the time between August and December, so that I could go to Germany in mid-August; I went straight down to Freiburg, where the Schröers took care of me in their Turnseestraße flat; Bruce and Maude went to the *Deutscher Kaiser*. And with the English Church just around the corner, Bruce and I were even able to go in for a kind of rehearsal, too.

The next day I went to the station in town to meet the von Richthofens' train, and travelled with them down to Littenweiler, which meant that I saw Frieda and her sisters together for the first time, and thought what a very good choice I had made, avoiding the severe though principled Else and the pleasure-loving, exuberantly cheerful and (to me) empty-headed Johanna; but though at least I travelled in the same cab as Frieda, I naturally could spend very little time with her. I went down to Littenweiler again the following day, but by then the whole establishment seemed devoted to sorting out clothes and hair dressings (or 'hair-do's' as they would now be called), and I felt very unnecessary.

The day after that was the wedding itself. It was a lovely day, from early on; and, in the morning, the Schröers drove me to the big peasant inn along Waldseestraße which was hosting the wedding breakfast before the church ceremony. The von Richthofens stayed in Littenweiler until the last minute, of course, and half the party – including Frieda – was late for the breakfast, which itself went on for so long that we had to depart in considerable haste for the church ceremony, which was back in Wiehre (here Arnold Schröer would be my best man). And then we all had to go up to Regina Buchholzer's place in the Münsterplatz for drinks and celebration, though the von

xxxviii

Richthofens were clearly rather displeased that we were not all going back down to Littenweiler and their place with the Blas sisters. But I had insisted on going to somewhere in town; I did not want to have to traipse all the way down to Littenweiler at half-past two, get there well after three, and then come all the way back into town again before five, the von Richthofens having insisted that the wedding should not take place until one o'clock, to allow friends and relations to come down to Freiburg during the morning. They had not bothered to find out from me that I had already booked the Bridal Suite at the Schweizerhof in Luzern for that night, and had reserved a compartment on the express down there, the only good train leaving at five from Freiburg, and taking a couple of hours.

So we met for our breakfast. It was a little odd to me that there was no restriction upon the bride and groom meeting before the ceremony, as there was in Britain even at that date, bad luck being sure to follow if one of the two were to catch a glimpse of the other before they were both safely in church. But when in Rome, etc. etc. Unfortunately I found Frieda far too overdressed to be beautiful, in a dress with a train that was slightly absurd; she was also wearing veils which almost completely hid her face from view until she had folded them back over her forehead; and even then they kept drooping down, to be pushed back up again. Her hair, too, was styled up into a confection (along with hat) which I did not dare touch. She and I had been sat side by side but the whole situation was far too formal for us to enjoy talking much together. It was actually easier for me to talk with the Frau Baronin, on my left; she was as unruffled as usual, only slightly put out that on her other side was my brother Bruce, who had no German at all, forcing her to thrust out towards him her heavy pronunciation of English words mixed with German, often with no apparent result (he found it almost impossible to understand her, and she took him for a good bit of an idiot). Luckily he could talk to Else, on *his* other side, and her English was pretty good. My sister Maude was put next to the Baron and took in her stride the various compliments he made her, without his noticing that she could not understand him, but then the Baron spent most of

xxxix

the time either eating or talking to Frieda; and Maude could be content with the excellent English of Arnold Schröer.

For my part, I had the strong sensation that I was marrying a perfect stranger, and I guess that Frieda may have felt the same – the difference between us being that such a thing worried me rather a lot, though it did not appear to worry her at all; she was embarked on an adventure which involved lots of people, and dressing up too, and in spite of her attire she radiated happiness at the sheer fun of it all.

The church ceremony, when we finally got to it, nearly half an hour late (there were many people waiting in the little church, doubtless tut-tutting as they waited), is something of which I have almost no recollection, except of hearing Frieda's strong accent when she said 'I vill' (in English: we were having a Church of England wedding ceremony, rather to the scandal of the Frau Baronin, who would have liked something Roman Catholic, and twice as long, with a celebration Mass in the middle of it). Afterwards we went back for champagne to the Buchholz place: and it was here that Frieda went upstairs and changed into her travelling clothes, and when I recognised her almost for the first time that day. There had been speeches and toasts, and I had made a short speech (carefully rehearsed). Then the Baron stood up and said how this marriage between Germany and England was again uniting the oldest of friends at a time when politicians etc., etc. (I confess I stopped listening around here, as I knew he would be getting on to the iniquities of politicians who had no idea about the army, and did not finance it properly, and that – in comparison with the British – the Germany army was woefully under-manned, etc. etc.) By far the best part of this event was the presentation to us of a so-called *Freiburger Zeitung*, full of jokes about me and Frieda, put together by Schröer and some of the students I had known. I've kept my fragile old copy of this, over the years, because of the very touching way in which Freiburg thus celebrated and remembered me – and because it *was* a wonderful day, in so many ways.

After all the palaver was over, I insisted on the cab leaving on time for the station. This bit of the day – because I had organised

xl

it – ran to time. But some of the family at least came to the station with us, and bought platform tickets and then stood on the platform waving, which was rather nice. By now I felt exhausted and extraordinary, out of this world with tiredness and strain but also with exhilaration. Frieda – well, once again I had no idea what she felt, except that she cuddled up to me very happily as we stood in the train's corridor with the window down as far as we could bring it, waving. In spite of her hat and hair, she felt terribly young, and I wondered – not for the first time – whether she did not find me terribly old. But I was not going to ask her that. I had my pride.

And then we were on our own, unfortunately in an enormous square private compartment which would have contained ten or twelve, and was not designed for people to be cuddly in it, although there were curtains on the windows to the corridor. We first sat opposite each other, both looking out of the window – but because of the design of the compartment we felt very cut off from each other. Eventually we both relaxed into our seats – and then felt so far off from each other as to need megaphones against the noise of the train, so I changed over so as to sit next to her, and anticipated a little more bodily affection than we had as yet been able to show. Frieda however appeared very sleepy and it struck me that, in order to be ready for our wedding breakfast at ten, she had probably had to be up at four or five in the morning, with her hair to be prepared and all the dressing and clothes arrangements which had to be done. And before long she was asleep, on my shoulder, of which I felt inordinately proud. I was happy about that; I woke her only as were pulling into Luzern.

xli

CHAPTER IX

For several months I had been anxious that Frieda knew as little about sex as I did, but could think of no way of either bridging over this difficulty or of addressing it directly. Neither of her sisters was married; I could not appeal to them. I did not imagine that her mother had said much to her, being as she was so angry with her husband most of the time (it had been at the wedding that I could see for the first time the distance she kept from him). Nor did it strike me that the Blas sisters would invite discussion on the subject. Frau Schröer was perhaps the only woman whom I might have asked to discuss the matter with Frieda; and she was now hundreds of miles away.

Finally we got to our hotel, but only briefly saw our room (our cases would of course be opened and our things stowed for us) before we were being escorted downstairs again for dinner. We dined in the best dining room: the Schweizerhof was very grand (I was determined to show that although the Weekleys were not rich, they knew what was expected on such occasions). Only then could we at last go upstairs together to our room, and throw ourselves into one of their great soft armchairs, with her – for the first time ever, I think – risking to sit on my knee.

Never had she been so close: I found her terribly exciting. And so I did my best to open an intimate conversation by saying, gently, 'You know, we are not really married yet' – with the intention of telling her what I knew, as (doubtless) she blushed and hid her face. But she came back at me with a laugh and her brilliant smile, saying 'Oh, I know!' This made me think that perhaps she *had* had some kind of previous sexual experience, so that things would not be too difficult after all. I had already wondered not just about all-girl boarding schools, and crushes among the *Backfische* there, but about all those ardent young soldiers in Metz whose company she had enjoyed, and whom she had doubtless kissed goodnight to, and whose erections she might perhaps have been conscious of, and whose names kept coming up during conversation during the breakfast and the hotel celebration. Anyway, at this point she seemed in no mood for any

xlii

further kind of conversation or enlightenment; so I simply told her, as we kissed gently, that when she felt like going to bed, I would go downstairs and would probably stay there for a bit, and drink a little. I wanted to make as easy as I could for her what I assumed would for her be the difficulty of getting into bed with a man who was still 'passing strange' to her. I thought I was giving her time to get herself washed, or whatever she did at night, undressing in her own closet, and there slipping into her 'nighty', as they are now apparently and rather horribly called.

In fact, as I learned over the next few days, all this was quite unnecessary; she did not in the least mind appearing in her 'undies' or showing at least her upper parts naked to me, and she was so far uninhibited as (to start with) not always to close the door when using the water closet. That was something however that I wanted changed; and change it did.

That night, however, I also wanted a drink, so was more than happy to go downstairs when she yawned and looked quizzically at me. I was very nervous, I remember – but more of coming to a climax too quickly when we started to make love than of not being able to make love at all. I wanted to calm down a bit, so applied myself to the crossword in the newspaper, and sipped my excellent brandy, while never for a second forgetting the excitement that waited for me upstairs. And waited; for perhaps half an hour. It would be no bad thing, I told myself, if she actually fell asleep before I came back up into the room: I was also not sure of getting undressed into bed under the enquiring gaze of a woman: something I had not done since I was about four years old.

When I finally judged the time was right, I went up and opened our room door, as gently as I could and in some trepidation, to discover a darkened room; but my first relieved thought, that she was already asleep, was interrupted by her deep, throaty chuckle from somewhere behind me. She could see much better in the dark than I could, coming into the dark from the lighted corridor as I was. I felt baffled; she was not on nor in the bed – that much I could discover and feel. I was actually slightly annoyed; why was she choosing this moment to play childish games with me – perhaps the most significant moment of our adult lives? 'Where

xliii

are you, my dearest Frieda', I called out, probably rather irritably. Again a giggle, from high-up behind me. I spun round, and fell over what I assumed to be a low table (it certainly hurt like one) as I did so: more laughter. I hated being humiliated like this, and groped back to the wall till at last I found the electric-light switch – everything up-to-date in the *Schweizerhof* – to observe her, in frilly knickers but not much else, sitting on a high cupboard and laughing like anything, her face almost split in half by her laugh. What *was* she playing at – I went across and, as she sprang into my arms, lifted her down, telling her to go to bed while I was in the closet (a friend at college had told me always to pee before making love, as it helped). And then I turned the light off again.

Holding her almost naked, however, brought me the most intense feelings of pleasure, but made my peeing afterwards terribly difficult: I had to hold myself almost horizontal in the closet, my erection was so stiff.

When I finally got naked into bed, she was actually in tears: 'I thought it would be such fun,' she said between sobs. But the very touch of her naked body was bringing me to climax and I quickly swathed myself in the sheet – just as well, as I found myself coming in floods at that moment. She, I think, had no idea of what was happening; but I was in no doubt that a little delay would be all for the best. As well as running my hands all over her – and she had hair between her legs, as I had been warned to expect – I began to explore her opening with my finger and was pleased to find it moist; I took this to mean that she was ready for me, even wanted me, and as soon as I was hard again I climbed on top of her and began to thrust into her. I had been told it might take a bit of doing, and I had the strong impression that there really ought to be an easier way to do it than this odd butting in which she took no part at all, except for keeping her knees around her chest. She did yelp a bit as I banged into her but quite quickly I came again, I think half in her at least, and paused. 'Was that it?' she asked. 'No,' I answered proudly, 'I'm not done yet!' For I knew I wasn't. So I banged on when I could and in the end I seemed to slip over the edge of something and felt I was either out of her or really in her. And I was in: and could thrust until I came for the third time. The

xliv

whole thing had taken no more than a quarter of an hour or twenty minutes, I am sure. She was gasping a bit and this time pulled away from me quickly. 'It hurts', she said. I tried to be comforting but found myself drifting away to sleep (it had been the most exhausting day); I tried to say good-night but am not quite sure whether I managed it.

In the morning the bed was quite a mess and – as for Frieda – she was rather subdued. She said nothing about the night; nor did I. But I was tremendously happy, and she looked wonderful. I am not going to describe here what she looked like, naked, though that is an image I shall carry with me to my dying day. I think that writing it down would however be vulgar (I can think of passages in friend Lawrence's fiction which convey very clearly how uninhibited *he* was in such matters: but, after all, vulgar comes from *vulgus*, the common people, so one can hardly be surprised).

All the same, the honeymoon was not much of a success. We were booked in for a week, and did all the dutiful Luzern things, going to the *Museggmauer* and walking the wooden bridges and looking at the lake in the evening under the lights, but what Frieda seemed to enjoy most was simply sitting by the window of our room with the trams rumbling by beneath, looking out over the trees to the lake beyond, with a novel in her hands; waiting for the next splendid meal.

As for me, the very sight of the Wasserturm in the middle of the Chapel Bridge was enough to remind me of what we were really here for. The days may have passed rather slowly, but the nights I can't speak of, as – two or three times every night and usually in the morning too – I fucked her.

I hope the reader will note, and appreciate, the ease and complacency which I here use this antique word, now employed by modernist writers of prose though still banned among the more anæmic classes. In the past forty years or so, indeed, writing, like government, has been wrested from the few and fit and has become a democratic occupation. Very few middle-class[3] people

---

[3]   *Middle-class* today is, I know, like *bourgeois* in being contempt-uously applied by 'intellectuals' to those who pay their way and look after their children.

xlv

'fucked' in 1899; I most certainly did not, and – because of the ban on the word – I later found myself unable to include it in my *Etymological Dictionary*, in spite of having all the necessary data and historical material ready prepared for it. My publisher simply forbade it. (The only consideration with which I could console myself was Sir James Murray's own confession of his sadness that, in the *New English Dictionary*, the word 'cunt' had been 'lost' only 'after wide consultation and much discussion'.)

But my work on the word 'fuck' brought me to something of the same state of mind as friend Lawrence seems to have reached in his essay 'A Propos' (though with him, it is always hard to tell what he really does think: his is not a mind given to clear expression). The word has not only been established as an intensive in the language of this country for four hundred years, but – while coarse – in its primary meaning has the inestimable advantage of going straight to the point. It describes something which the euphemisms always leave vague. 'Making love to' can mean anything from 'gazing adoringly' to 'fucking from arsehole to breakfast-time' as the saying goes; 'go to bed with', again describes without in the least describing. I wish to say here no more than that Frieda was thoroughly fucked and would be pregnant within a month; but that I will hereafter in this narrative use the word with some restraint, as by no means always appropriate, in spite of the practice of my literary contemporaries.

What Frieda actually thought of all this sexual activity I did not know at the time, though I can now guess; she said not a thing, during these early years, except sometimes to say 'not now' or 'no, Tante Rosa'. This did not disturb me; she did not seem to me as if she found it very repellent, and at times she was a very active partner indeed, liking to sit on top of me and to be underneath in various ways, being explored there too. She did not, however, do much in the way of exploring me, which I would have enjoyed. Looking back, I should probably have asked her more about what she liked, and have told her what *I* liked. But I was not accustomed to do such a thing in 1899, any more than the huge majority of husbands were. Sexual pedants like Marie Stopes, telling men what to do, did not exist. I would have had to have been a very

xlvi

different kind of person. And she was certainly pleased to be pregnant, and to have children, so in that way she accepted her part of the sexual bargain. At least, so I thought; but I suspect I did not *think* so much as simply continue to do what I most thoroughly wanted. And I did want. Oh yes, how I wanted. What really stuffed my bag, I discovered, was fucking her two or three times, from all angles (let the reader consider what that might mean, and reckon that it probably *does* mean that), and then having her curl up on my shoulder and fall asleep.

But, in her, I had found the thing in life which turned out to make everything else worthwhile, something which I had never known before. Loving her and making love to her made sense of everything, in ways I did not need to think about. I was simply overwhelmingly happy, and that happiness spilled over into everything I did. And she was the wonderful woman who had opened up this life to me; and I had naturally no idea that anything would ever change. This was how we would grow old, for sure (though, again, I guess that Frieda thought less about growing old than I did).

xlvii

CHAPTER X

Marriage for me was thus, to begin with, a perpetual state of happiness and contentment (on the one side) and (on the other) of excitement at the fact that I was not only permitted but was required, as a marital duty, to ravish this marvellous female, over and over: which was exactly what I hugely desired to do. It was the result of my non-stop love-making during September 1899, I am sure, that Monty was born nine months later, in June 1900. I then – according to the best advice of my doctor friend James Callow – allowed a three or four month pause, as I would after each birth – and then I started again, resulting in the births of Elsa in September 1902 and Barbara in October 1904.

These early years were very special, however. We had moved into our first, narrow little Nottingham double house (today, vulgar people – I can name friend Lawrence[4] – would say 'semi-detached') in New Basford, where every morning I would leap on to the bus which ran past our door, taking me down to the University. One thing I recall was the moment which might in fact have been a disaster, when Frieda managed not just to slide and slither down the stairs (pregnant with Monty at the time, though very early on), and somehow was able to do so in an extraordinary series of thumps and crashes which concluded with her sitting at the bottom of the stairs, quite unhurt but extensively bruised, poor thing. I had run out of my study when the noise started, but could only look at her sitting there and say gently 'Have I married Johanna Frieda von Richthofen or an earthquake?' To which she nodded and smiled hugely, and laughed 'beides!' I demanded to see the damage, just in case, and in our bedroom enjoyed full inspection of parts usually unseen in daylight, with thoroughly pleasing consequences for us both. We were so loving together. Or so I thought.

Our houses alone, as we moved up the scale of properties, will tell you about the hard and successful work I did in those first

---

[4]   See *Lady Chatterley's Lover*, chap. 11: 'new little streets of semi-detacheds were run up, very desirable!'

xlviii

years in Nottingham, somehow managing to combine everything – not just setting up a Department of Languages, but running the commercial classes, lecturing three evenings a week for the University extension classes, writing that primer of French Literature for Blackie, continuing to produce my series of French teaching books for Clive, and lecturing in the summer in Cambridge. All of which increased my income so that by 1900, in time for the birth of Monty, we could afford to move out of a house which even I would confess to have been a little small and perhaps poky, into the rather grander double house in Goldswong Terrace (higher ceilings, a front garden, nearer to the College, *not* on the noisy cab and bus route), and with generally nicer neighbours. Frieda was on her own a good deal during this period, though she read a great deal more than ever before, in her life: I brought her books to read like *Le Rouge et le Noir* and asked her what she thought of them. But as soon as she was pregnant, life looked up for her too. Elsa would be born next, and though I recall that at first she seemed to resemble facially that august vieillard ex-president Krüger, she grew much prettier. Two years later, we could move again, into a very trim and nice house in Vickers Street: once again a double house, but larger all round, as fitting our growing family (Barbara was born here in 1904). And everything I did, everything I thought, everywhere I went, was for Frieda; I tried to fulfil her lightest wish; and while we were married, the world didn't hold another woman for me.

But it was soon after the birth of Barbara, around Christmas-time, that Stafford took me on one side and said that it would not be entirely safe for Frieda to have any more children, so he was relying on me to be careful in that respect. What a disaster! That was the ending of uninhibited sex; that was the ending of that spontaneous, untroubled, underlying happiness to which I had at last grown accustomed, and which I loved. I could and did at times use a condom, but I always hated it (the disgusting smell, the worse than disgusting feel, the necessary preparation spoiling any possibility of spontaneous lust; apart from that there was just the occasional Saturday night with her when Tante Rosa was visiting: and *that* was bloody fucking that . . . in every sense. It was a huge

xlix

change; I never felt again that great surge of confidence and well-being and optimism I had enjoyed in the first years of our marriage. A whole component of my happiness had been struck out, with sex being at weekends, once a month, if I were lucky. But at least other things were going well. The children were growing up, extremely beautiful children too; and with our doctor Stafford's help we had acquired as a nurse the good child Ida Wilhelmy, only fifteen years old, rescued from the Flersheims in the Park where she had been so miserable. And then, with our cook Bertha, who also loved children, our routines and rôles as parents were beautifully established. I was also able to prevail on the University College authorities during 1904-05 to establish something at that date unique, I think, in the British University system: two posts of *Lektor* (one French, one German) in my Department, the German one going to the young Ernst Stahl in 1906. They were immediately copied by Universities the country over: the idea of getting as teachers in Modern Languages native speakers who were, all the same, not fully qualified – and therefore cheap – was overwhelmingly attractive. But at least I had been able to establish contacts where I was known, and could ensure a regular supply of super-qualified *Lektor*s from the Sorbonne, Bern and Freiburg, which did a good deal to put the University College on the map.

And I can also bridge over from my first vivid awareness (and love) of language, which started around the age of eight, to my first little book on the subject, which I began when I was aged forty-three, in 1908, and had the idea of dedicating to my beloved, necessary wife. I put it together over three years, with no idea of how I might bring it all to completion; a labour of love for her if ever there was one. It contained all my finest examples of how English words had their roots deep in French and German – for example, how *belfry* is always thought by English people to be the place where bells are hung, though the word comes from the Old French *berfroi*, a tower used in warfare – and *that* in turn comes from two German words, represented by modern German *bergen* (to hide or guard) and *Friede* (peace), so that it means 'guard-peace'. And that made me think too of *Frieda*, the un-peaceful,

1

the earthquake personified, the totally loved.

My God, the irony to me now of working so hard at that book, my book for her as it was always meant to be. Following the advice of my publisher, when published it was a great deal shorter than originally planned, and given the rather racier title of *The Romance of Words*. I had always thought of it as a kind of dictionary, to be called something like *An Etymological Glossary of Foreign Elements in the English Language*, but John Murray had been strongly against that title – indeed that whole conception of the book – from the start. Nevertheless it had always been my book for her, finished (as it turned out) at the very moment when she was planning to leave me.

For I put the last words to the manuscript of the book (the *belfry* example included, in the chapter I had come to call 'Wrong Association') in January 1912, at the end of the Christmas holidays, at the start of that terrible year; but when I was done, the whole enterprise seemed so inadequate to me, compared with the great *Glossary* or *Dictionary of Etymology* which I had always planned to write, that I could not bear to include in it the dedication to Frieda which I had always hoped to add. That would have to wait, I thought, until I *did* write the *Dictionary* – or perhaps the *Dictionary of English Surnames* which had also become a great project. But at least I held a copy of *The Romance of Words* in my hands on 1 March 1912: and I presented it to her, proudly. I wrote the date in it, along with words for its presentation, in the copy which I still possess – it being, oddly, something she failed to take with her when she left.

Murray was a great publisher, and I was very lucky to have found him: Blackie would not have done half so well for such a book, or for its multitude of successors. Murray was a serious individual who nevertheless very well understood the market, and who had contacts in America, too, so that there was an almost simultaneous publication of the book there. It was my first book with him; and after some excellent reviews, its sales burgeoned, so that it was reprinted in June, proving him entirely right about the title and the scope of the book. It may have been small in size but it was packed with thirty years of thinking and experience: and

li

I went on revising it, so that it grew better and better. And there was I, not thinking it good enough to include a dedication to Frieda in it. As a result she never had a book dedicated to her; but I rather doubt whether she would have taken it with her, even if it had contained a dedication.

For, that same year, in the period between the book's actual arrival in March and the reprint in June, and without my doing anything to provoke it, she destroyed our marriage, our household, our happiness, our children's upbringing, my peace of mind, the comfortable old age of my parents, my relationship with her parents, my own carefully-built reputation in Nottingham, my future career, and every bit of pleasure in the writing which I had done. *The Romance* – how I came to hate that title! I use it here only in deep sarcasm – had been my first venture into the field of popular publication, but I quickly grew certain that I would never again be able to do anything, let alone the big, serious books I had always planned. Beside me sat a spectre, inhibiting all my future work; it felt like the end of my career, and of the future for which I had spent so many years preparing and working. All tossed away, in just a few weeks, by someone who did not care for any of the things which mattered to me: or for me either, if it came to that.

CHAPTER XI

So when did the trouble really start? Well, one way of reckoning would say late in July 1898, when I first clapped eyes on her (but, clearly, never for a moment understood her). Another reckoning would say Tuesday 30 April 1912, the day on which, to my utter astonishment, she told me that though she had been married to me for twelve and a half years, she had been betraying me for most of that time. But yet another reckoning would supply the date of 3 March 1912: just a couple of days after the first copies of *The Romance of Words* had arrived, and when I had unthinkingly invited a young puppy to lunch, who proceeded to assist my wife in wrecking my life.

I shall start with him. I could sum him up – as I once did 'genius' – as someone who finds it necessary to give convincing proof of his genius by trampling underfoot all the received conventions of decency and morality. I had seen him sitting at the back of the theatre in College lectures a few years earlier: never knew his name, but remembered him as a scrawny little lout, bright hair, bulbous nose, high collar, little ginger moustache, and a high-pitched laugh, which he did not always employ in the places I wanted it. But I never knew him. All those people saying he was a student of mine! Young Mr Lawrence was not even doing a degree course; he was going straight into elementary school teaching. He did not look like the kind of young man who was going to command the attention of his children, either. But it takes all sorts. 'Food for powder, food for powder': elementary teachers good and bad are simply necessary, as are teachers in general. I should know.

I also knew my real students, the ones utterly unlike him, those following degree courses: the ones who trusted me, the ones I trusted, as I know and trust them right down to this day. I count myself lucky in them. *I* was a good student, and I always encouraged those who seemed to me not just able but prepared to dedicate themselves to their work, as I knew I had done. To judge by the marks he acquired at the end of his courses, young Mr Lawrence seems to have done what he was obliged to, and not a

liii

stroke more, so that he could spend the rest of his time chasing women and scribbling interminable poems and novels.

But then, out of the blue, at the end of February 1912 comes this letter from someone at first unknown, who had once, he said, sat in my classes, and who was soon going to Germany: and could I give him any advice about getting teaching work there? Name of Lawrence: and that certainly rang a bell – there had been an ex-Nottingham student whose poetry had of late been taken up by at least one rather prestigious literary magazine, and who had also had a novel published. Not many of those, I can tell you, coming out of the Normal programme at the University College. Without knowing it, I had had a genius in my class: and I had never even known who it was.

After I had made this connection, we asked him to lunch on Sunday 24 February (the date is in my old diary) but he wrote saying that he couldn't come as he had 'another appointment'. I was not especially bothered, simply wondering what prior appointment might take precedence over that with a Professor whom one wanted to help with one's career – but Frieda was disappointed not to meet this brilliant young poet and novelist (her sentiments, not mine), and wrote asking him again, for a week later. And that he deigned to manage. He did not, however, seem to know that 'lunch' meant twelve thirty for one o'clock. That morning (I confess I had got up extremely late, as was then my wont) I had poor Claude Gilli's 'Key' to my *Senior French Course* to revise and knock into shape, and was hard at work, only coming out of my study when I heard the noise of the dinner gong at one sharp, having heard no door bell and thinking that no visitor had yet arrived – to find that Lawrence had been in the house for almost an hour and had spent it talking to Frieda. He had never rung at the front door at all but, seeing her in the garden with the children, had made his entrance through the garden gate: they had been out there at first because it was the most beautiful weather, a day like April, sunny and warm.

Over lunch, Lawrence gave away at once the fact that he had no idea about education or about Germany. He actually thought he might be able to walk into a job as a *Lektor* in a Germany

liv

University on the strength of a really-not-especially-distinguished two-year elementary teacher training qualification, and three years at the coal-face (appropriate location for him, of course) of an elementary school somewhere deep in the London suburbs. I asked him if he had ever considered following the degree course at the College, and he replied that he had started it but had then given it up. A pretty clear indication, I thought, that he was exactly the sort of student whose career should not expect much tender loving-kindness from me: but here he was, at the age of twenty-six, almost unqualified, fantasising about University teaching. At that age (which I did not tell him, though I was tempted to) I had been four years past my BA qualification, was in post as a full-time tutor at the University Correspondence College, and was pursuing the MA degree which I was awarded when I was twenty-seven. Getting a post as a *Lektor* at Freiburg was something possible only with my MA and my scholarship at Trinity, Cambridge, under my belt.

So my first job, over lunch, was to counsel Lawrence that he had very little chance (meaning not a chance in hell) of such a post. He was, however, an intelligent young man, if not a disciplined one, with a considerable talent for mocking impersonation, a talent I heard exercised on some of my colleagues during that luncheon (I did naturally wonder what his version of me would have been like). In passing he mentioned the novel he had recently published. I did not overwhelm him with the fact that I had, so far, something like nineteen books published (not counting the teachers' 'Key' books which went with a lot of them), and that they brought me in comfortably an extra two hundred a year. All I could really do for him was say that if ever he went to Freiburg (something pretty unlikely, as he was headed up into the Rhineland to stay with some cousins or other) he should knock on the door of the Schröer family and hand in the note of introduction which – back in my study for a moment – I scribbled out for him there and then and stuck in an envelope. When I got back to the dining room it was clear that he and Frieda were once again engaged in animated conversation – a conversation broken off as I came in. 'And what was that about?' I asked, genially. 'Ach, about Siegmund Freud

lv

and Oedipus', said Frieda, and Lawrence at once said 'I've never read him – but that doesn't stop me being interested.' 'I've not read him either', I replied, 'but from what my wife tells me about him I rather doubt if I shall.' Frieda's eyes blazed at me for a second, but then she joined me in wishing our visitor farewell and *auf Wiedersehen*.

It was Ida – who had joined us in the hall when Lawrence was preparing to set off – who also put it best: 'A person like that should not wear patent leather shoes,' she said, as Lawrence walked away down the drive. She knew at once what class he came from, and how he gave away his ignorance of middle-class manners by wearing such shoes for a lunch-time appointment. He obviously thought that a visit to the house of a Professor demanded finery, and they were the only finery he had. Well, good luck to him in Germany, I thought, hopeful, shiny-footed Mr Lawrence.

CHAPTER XII

I thought very little more about the visit. A couple of days later he sent Frieda a little note thanking us for our hospitality. And that – at first – was that. If I must be honest, I did not notice any change in Frieda's behaviour or manner; I made my usual Saturday night visit to her bedroom and bed, when she was neither more nor less welcoming than usual.

March went on pretty uneventfully, after the brilliant weather at its start, and April came into focus as the time for her usual visit to Germany – but this year for a very special reason, and one which precluded her taking either of the girls with her, though Barby had clamoured to go. Her father was celebrating fifty years in that experimental machine of discipline and inhumanity, the Prussian army (something which, so far as I was concerned, was constantly adding new horrors to the half-mechanical age in which we live); and there would be family gatherings to match, combined with massive overcrowding in the Montigny apartment. I had naturally been invited but, thank God, I was not able to go (it clashed with a rather important Senate meeting and vote).

But one or two odd things did happen. On one occasion, Frieda was not at home when I got back for dinner at night – and even Ida had no idea where her mistress was. Such a thing was almost unknown. Eventually she got back, full of excuses: trains were disrupted still, after the strike earlier in the year: she had been to see the Bradleys' old mother, out at Ilkeston. But then, sometime in the first half of April, when I got back unexpectedly early from Cambridge one Saturday evening, I was most surprised to find the Lawrence fellow in the house, although it was ten at night. Frieda explained that he had just knocked on the door, asking if she had time for some German conversation, before his trip, but I was shocked to find her with such a visitor at such a time, and got him out of the house as soon as I decently could. When he had gone, I told Frieda that I thought he was imposing far too much upon her and that she should refuse to see him in the future. I never suspected her of anything, however; never dreamed that she might be having an affair.

lvii

All was arranged for her to travel over on Thursday 2 May until, ten days or so before leaving, she suddenly announced that she wanted to travel on the Friday. My eyebrows doubtless expressed a question for surprise – tickets would have to be re-ticketed, reservations re-reserved. She did not explain, and I put it down to her not wanting to spend so long in the crowded bosom of her family – something I perfectly well understood. I did not imagine that it was because she wished to spend more time in Nottingham with me.

I had my usual University Extension lecture on the Monday evening of that week and got home very late, as ever; Frieda had as usual been waiting up for me, but also as usual took herself off to bed very soon after I had got home and had briefly told her about the evening. That was normal. During the Tuesday – one of the days I could spend mostly at home – she was rather tense, I thought (planning, I guessed, and worrying about which hat she could wear and which she should take). But after supper, and after all children had been put to bed, she came into my study and said she had something important she needed to say. Such a careful announcement was most unusual – she usually just burst out with what was on her mind, at breakfast or whenever – so I laid down my book and gave her my full attention, imagining it would be something about the house or about the children that needed to be taken care of while she was gone.

She said (I believe I can quote her exactly): 'I think you ought to know that I have not always been faithful to you.' I did not exactly take in what I was hearing: I thought it the prelude to some kind of joke – that she had been faithless to me in buying a dress made of material which I had criticised when I had seen it in the hands of her dressmaker, or something like that. I smiled and said 'Meaning?'

'Well: I have had lovers: men who loved me.'

'Who?'

'Your friend Dowson was one.'

I felt the solid floor rock beneath my chair. I had not seen much of Will of late – his lace business had needed all his attention, and I too had been at full stretch, as always. But this was staggering.

lviii

My first thought was that Frieda had somehow been taken ill; that this was delirium, and that she did not mean what she was saying. I stupidly asked her 'When?'

'Soon after Barby was born. He took me out in his car. We made love in the woods.'

She said this freely, and without apparently any shame or inhibition. But it was all utterly new to me. I must have stared without comprehension. I do not think that at this stage I was angry, or even jealous. It sounded like a report from another world, one in which I had never lived, and about which I was hearing for the first time. If anything, at this stage it was fascinating: as interesting as wondering what might happen in the next chapter of a good book. I asked a question, more to keep up my end of the conversation than for any better reason.

'And was he the only one? Your only lover?'

'No.'

'So who else?'

I did not know what I was expecting: the names of half my colleagues, or that of the Kurt-von-something man, or her bursting into laughter and giggles.

'Otto Gross.'

'The Freudian you told me about – the crazy one?'

'He was Else's lover before he was mine. He is the father of Else's boy Peter.' And she started to cry.

I still did not know what I was hearing, though I had the odd thought that *I* ought to be the one bursting into tears, not her. But Gross! Gross in every sense then. A new thought came to me: an explanation.

'So you are seeing him in Germany next week?'

'Of course not!'

And she ran out of the room, gulping with sobs.

The rest of the evening was . . . simply the rest of the evening. I did not see her again. When I finally came out of my study, after doing little else than stare at the wall for an hour, I saw Ida on the stairs (I rather think she was hanging about waiting for me) and she said that Frieda had gone to bed and that the children were all still asleep, and that everything was fine. She seemed to want to reassure me; I must have looked wild-eyed.

But here was my marriage potentially in ruins, and Frieda had gone to bed: and she would be leaving for the continent on Thursday afternoon. And I had a heavy day at the College tomorrow. Should I go and wake her up? But for what? To hear details? Those I certainly did not want. To plan the future? I was still too numb to think beyond the next ten minutes. It was half-past ten. I too must go to bed: I felt suddenly exhausted, though my mind was whirling. I had a whisky, the bottle rattling in the glass as I poured. It did, I think, nothing to calm me.

PROOFS EW ARWW 5-6 Feb.1939

CHAPTER XIII

I did however sleep better that night than for the next two weeks. It was, so far as I know, an utterly exhausted and dreamless sleep: nothing there for the delectation of Dr Freud. I did not see Frieda at breakfast, only the girls and Ida. She was obviously staying upstairs and avoiding me. I left for College, as I had to, at twenty-five past eight, but left a message that I would be home between five and six.

It was a tiring day, work first, and then my usual hour of golf with Kipping out at Hollinwell, and then back to work; even a cheerful exchange with my friend the busman on the way home brought me back in no mood for anything except supper. Frieda actually got back even later than I did, as she had been visiting the Bradleys, over in the Park. That was, if anything, a danger-sign; I reckoned they had always been a bad influence on her, the two girls in particular being full of wild schemes and plans. I suspected that she had been talking about our conversation of the previous evening.

But what in fact happened on the evening of the Wednesday was that I had the biggest row of my life – with Frieda, or with anyone, ever; and that it rumbled and grumbled and snarled on for hours, with intervals in which we sat down, walked round the house; or went completely quiet, when a child appeared, or when it was time to kiss it goodnight; and then confronted each other again, resuming our savage sniping and quarrelling. And constantly walking out of the room; and then walking back in. And the evening ended with an episode of which even now I am a little ashamed.

I started by asking Frieda – in English, by now usually the language for us of serious exchanges – if she had anything more to tell me. She asked me what I meant.

'The names of any other lovers, I mean.'

'Is it the number which matter to you?'

'"Matters", not "matter": it's a singular noun.'

'I hate your bloody English, I hate you, I hate England, and I would like never to see any of *you* ever again, and never use this

lxi

bloody language again.' And she carried on in German, as I did too. It was time, I thought, to bring an end to the preliminaries and go for the important things: like abject apologies from her, and discussion about how we were to go on, if it all. I wanted some show, at least, of humiliation from her. I started off:

'You go off betraying me with man after man and all you do is complain about the English! They have nothing to do with it. Good God, you have been breaking your marriage vows with impunity, treating me as a trusting fool, disgracing your family, your children and my parents . . . and yet *you* are the one who complains. Don't you even want to say that you are sorry?'

'Well I know very well that you never loved me. Not really. It was never any good between us. I loved you very much, and you just took me for granted.'

'I've always loved you, from the first moment I saw you, *malheureusement*.'

'No, you never did; you never loved as *I* mean loved. You kneeled down and adored me, you never loved me. You did not respond to *me*.'

And then Ida knocked: Elsa was going to bed and had to be kissed. A pause – and then to it, again. I lashed back:

'You *always* wanted to be adored: and I gave you everything I had; you had your own way, always! I was faithful to you from the day I saw you – and before that. You might have called me a model husband. I suppose that was my fault. You had better put on my tombstone "He was a poor fool and a good husband." I was as near to you as ever you'd let me come.' And – before she could deny this – 'I know the truth is unimportant to you.'

'But truly I wanted love, not adoration.'

'Bosh. I thought I had a wife. I gave you everything I had: my love, my life, everything. You were my life, but sadly that seems not to be worth the stump of a cigarette to you, when it comes to it. I should have killed myself rather than have allowed myself to love you or to marry you. And you have still not had the decency to apologise even once.'

And somewhere around here she started calling me 'sad': 'Sadly! You are so right, you stupid, sad, resigned, self-pitying

lxii

man! Sad is right: you have always been sad. You are a sad case altogether, you great Professor Weekley, I really understand that now, but in fact I have known it for many years. And all your frantic love-making has never meant anything to me at all.'

And so on, for hours. Constant attacks, constant retaliations, both of us doing all we could to hurt the other. I was surprised at her: I think she was surprised at me, too. I accused her of saying that my life was a lie and a falsity. She told me, I think, that sex with me had never been any good, and never would be any good, and I accused her of being a whore with her legs always open, always ready for it, from me or from anyone. And then she had to go and kiss Montague good-night, and I gulped down a quick drink. And then back to the bad-tempered fray. It all came to an end when I accused her of going off to Germany the next day to have her paramours (not a word she would ever have used) with impunity, and she swore over and over that she had no lovers in Germany but that she now wanted never to see me again, she was an independent woman with her own needs (I broke in to say that I found her needs disgusting – 'but what is a little dirt to you, hey?') But she struck me as like Mr Micawber as she swore that she loved her children and would never abandon them.

And she repeated that if I had ever 'really' loved her she would never have taken lovers in the first place, so that it was really all my fault, and I started to shout that she had never been anything but a degenerate at heart and in her soul – but then I kept my voice down, thinking of Ida and the children. And so we went on, until I told her that she was a terrible mother and did not deserve to have children, so that it would be a good thing if she abandoned them for good and all, and she swore at me – I think she used the 'Arsch' word – and stormed out.

One of the things that happened to me during this quarrel was most peculiar. I found myself getting rather aroused, sexually. I am to some extent ashamed of this but at the time it was irresistible. I gave her a few minutes to get to her room and then followed her up, knocked and in the same movement opened the door and went in. What followed even I hesitate to write down here; let me simply say that I wanted something of what those

lxiii

others had been getting, and it ended up with my fucking her almost without preparation, in spite of the fact that she felt drier than I had ever known her. She did not much protest (just a few grunts of 'that hurts!') but I could also tell how angry and detached from it all she was. I came rather quickly and pulled out almost at once, and then left as fast as I could. I knew my desire was empowered by rage, not by love; but rage and lust are close cousins. Or so I learned that night.

This was the Wednesday night. I had arranged a light day at the University for the Thursday morning so that I could come home for lunch, and to do most of my work after she had left for London. I now felt extremely anxious about having possibly alienated her, in taking advantage of her in bed like that; it might result, I thought, in her being so angry as to encourage her to go off with the girls not just to London but to Germany. I actually feared that I might never see them again. But I couldn't go to London with her, to make sure she took the girls only up to Hampstead, to my parents; there was a very important Departmental meeting at 2.30 which I simply had to chair. And I did not want to tell her I was worried, in case it gave her the idea of actually doing what I only feared. So on the Thursday morning I tried to press on her the idea that Ida should go with her, but she saw through my plan immediately.

'I shall not take the girls to Germany, of course I won't; there would be no room for them in the house, and there will be nowhere for them to stay with me. Otherwise I certainly would take them, to get them away from you and from this blooooody England and the blooooody influences of it. Don't be frightened, you will see your children again, just as soon as you take some time off from this wretched work that keeps you at your desk day and night, and you think more of me than as someone you simply assault, wanting sex just when you feel like it, and instead pay some real attention to me and to those around you; to people who are not connected with the College or your everlasting books. That would be a surprise for us all. It is for example months since you even saw your parents, you always say you are too busy, but always you take them for granted, all the time. Just as you take *me*

lxiv

for granted, all the time, like last night.'

I now however felt sure that she was going off to see a man; that was, for me, the single most important fact about all these exchanges. Why else had she made that announcement two days before? Why tell me about lovers, if there was not one in the offing? Why had she changed the date of her travels? I asked her about it over and over again and she denied that there was anyone waiting for her in Germany. She would be staying overnight with my parents – but could she have arranged to meet someone in London? I got her on her own for a moment and challenged her with that idea. She swore at me as 'Du alter Arsch!' (her father being in the military had left its traces, I thought in passing) and said it was a ridiculous idea.

At the University, that morning, I took the opportunity to make a telephone call to Will Dowson, at his firm; I wanted to know where he was (to be exact, I pretended I wished to see him on Friday). His secretary, or telephone operator, was however afraid that I could not see him until the week after next. He was away: 'Abroad', she said, 'I think in Germany.' That made me certain that Frieda was meeting him.

We had a wretched luncheon, early, so that she could get off to catch the train; and in front of the children we tried to behave normally, neither of us wanting to. I found not a moment available for challenging her about Dowson. And eventually the cab came, and Frieda and the girls and Ida piled in; Ida was accompanying them to the station (my sister would be meeting the train at King's Cross). I had to go off to the College, but as I walked to the bus I was in my head saying all the things I really wanted to say to her and composing the letter which I now intended to send to her to Metz. It did not differ much from the one I actually sent that evening (which must be the Thursday, the 2nd: but I got very confused about dates, around now: even the month of the year).

> I am afraid I am quite unable to believe your assertion that you have no lover, either waiting for you in Germany or being met on your way there. I believe your visit is a way of meeting him, as you

lxv

almost told me two days ago. If this is indeed the case, then you must understand that our marriage is at an end. You cannot expect that it would continue.

I still cannot understand what has happened. I would have died for you! But I fear you are with Dowson as I know he is in Germany. I wish you to wire me as soon as you get this: if it is true that you have been with him, or will soon be with him, you are to wire to me 'GANZ RECENT'.

I would nevertheless wish you, as ever, to convey my respects to your parents. Your still-loving husband

Ernst

PROOFS EW ARWW 5-6 Feb.1939

CHAPTER XIV

I have never forgotten the weekend which followed. Ida was away for what had been arranged as a short holiday (she was going to the East Coast with a friend); Bertha was away as usual, the first Sunday in the month, with the Saturday off too as a treat. There was only Monty in the house and I was determined to give him no clue as to what I was feeling; but when on the Friday he told me that a school friend of his wanted to go to Derby with *his* father on the Saturday, and would he be allowed to stay overnight at his friend's house, both before and after their trip, I jumped at the chance and gave him full permission.

I then spent the weekend raging around the house; I slept at odd hours, then got up and resumed pacing. I do not remember eating. I scrawled out letters, one after another, madly, to Will Dowson, to Otto Gross, to Frieda, to Papa and Mama, to my own father and mother, to Maude, another one to Frieda, to George, to Bruce, to Else, to Johanna, yet another to Frieda; wrote them all out but (thank God) never sent any of them. I remember going into Frieda's room, and opening her wardrobe, and hiding my face, smeared with tears, against her clothes: the blouses and dresses I knew so well, all still impregnated with the scent of her, the marvellous woman she was, the woman I would happily have been tortured for: but a woman who was now quite deliberately tearing me to pieces, throwing me away as no more important than the paper wrapping off a parcel. It was all so wrong: so utterly unfair. What more could I have done? How could I have treated her better?

Everything reminded me of her, and of the things we had done together and the places we had been. Even the Tinworth panel in my room, which we had bought when we had very little money indeed but when she – seeing my love for it – had poured out into my hands the whole contents of her purse, as her contribution . . . and the chess set in the corner where I had tried to teach her chess but she had cried at failing to be better at it, and I had comforted her . . . and the piano where she had so often played and sung in her own lovely if unrhythmical style.

PROOFS EW ARWW 5-6 Feb.1939

But the uncertainty, as so often, turned out to be even worse than the hurt and pain that came with betrayal. Was my marriage at an end or not? I knew that, in spite of all my flashings of hatred, underneath I loved and wanted her enough to take her back – if she were not with Dowson, if she would come. I wanted her as my wife. I wanted my wife.

I expected a telegram from her on the Saturday, or at latest on the Sunday. Nothing came. That made it much worse. The fact that she was not wiring me must mean that she was considering her answer – or really was not coming back. Or could it be that she had never got my letter? Could it have been mislaid in the teeming von Richthofen house that weekend? Or was so deeply into her affair that she ignored such a thing as my letter. Or was not in Metz at all. On the Monday – still nothing. So she was off with Dowson somewhere. I had to go to work. Goodness knows how I survived the day or the Senate meeting I had to attend: I had hardly slept, I had hardly eaten (just some stale bread I found). When I got back, Ida and Bertha were at home again; but there was no telegram. In a rage I sat down and wrote to her father, and got Ida to run to the box to catch the 6.45 p.m. collection. With luck, that would arrive on Wednesday morning. I wrote something like this:

> 6 May 1912
> Dear Papa!
> Congratulations on your festive day!
>
> I sent Frieda a very important letter on Thursday asking her to wire me at once, but she has still not answered. Could you tell her to do so immediately. Things are not, I am afraid, altogether good between us, but I hope for a better future.
> > Your loving son
> > Ernst

I reckoned that if he got this on Wednesday, then at the very latest I would hear something by the Friday; I also hoped that it would at least make him talk seriously to Frieda (I was and always had been his favourite son-in-law).

I got back exhausted on the Tuesday evening, however, to find a telegram waiting for me. I could hardly bear to open it. 'G A N S R E C E N T' [*sic*] it said: the worst possible (also absurd) words. I felt maddened at the simple impertinence of it, though the words were the ones I had chosen for her (or nearly). So Dowson *was* there with her, as I had suspected! I had a telegram form to hand, in my study, and sent Ida down the road with it, filled in as 'K E I N E M O E G L I C H K E I T' – very short but clear enough (I was worried that Ida – and any of the folk in Metz – might comprehend if I were more explicit).

So that apparently was that. All the years of my marriage, of working, working, working so that we could live up to a bit of the style which my own personal Freiin von Richthofen expected; all my years of devotion, the huge love and devotion of my parents, the love of her parents – all thrown away for the sake not just of another man, but my own best friend. And the children now motherless as a result.

How could she: I had been betrayed, betrayed, betrayed, taken for a simple fool, and taken advantage of over and over again. And it had been a long, cold betrayal, over a period of years, too. She must have laughed at me. I could hear Will Dowson laughing at me, just as he always had. I wondered immediately whether, if ever he came back, I would go round to his house and confront him, tell him how much I despised him and then hit him as hard as I could.

And so be accused of assault? The newspapers would love it. 'Professor attacks friend: *crime passionnel*!!'

Or would she make a life abroad with Dowson, and neither of them ever come back? He couldn't do that! He had a business to run.

I spent all that night lying awake with a much worse 'dismal headache' than anything Gilbert could ever have imagined, going over and over what it would be best to do, sleep utterly 'taboo'd by anxiety'. I would certainly confront Dowson when he got back (if he came back), to give him a piece of my mind as violently as I could, using any language I could indulge in, not caring a damn

lxix

about impropriety; I could also imagine hitting him hard in the stomach and winding him, but not so badly that he could accuse me of assault. I would incidentally also inform him that he was no longer Barbara's godfather.

What Frieda had engaged in with Otto Gross had confirmed all my hatred of psychoanalysts, of (so called) Freudians: of their constant moral of 'sleep with your patients', sex being thought the answer to everything. There were moments when I hoped never to see Frieda again; but I also wanted to see her, if only so as to hit her too, in that wide mouth of hers, to make her feel just a little of the pain I was feeling. Perfectly inconsistently, I also wanted her back, desperately, because I loved her so much in spite of everything, and in spite of hating her too. I wanted our life to go on just as it had been. There's that poem by the late Edward Eastaway, 'First known when lost'. That's what I felt. I couldn't work, I had deadlines approaching (not only was there Gilli's work to go over once again, I had promised to prepare a revised and enlarged second edition of *The Romance of Words* – and the irony of that title, coming out just then, struck me yet again). I felt utterly helpless and useless. I wanted simply to go back to where we had been. It could not be that my awful love-making on that last Wednesday could mark the end of our sexual life together; that would be unbearable.

What to do?

I had to do something, even if it were only a feint, a pretence. I worked out a plan. Planning for the children looked as it were the only sane point of departure. It was also the only thing that Frieda would expect me to do, but she would more than anything else hate the thought of *her* children being taken away from her. That would surely make her come back. Neither she nor I would have wanted them in the families of either of my married brothers. So for the moment my sister Maude must be their mother, along with help from my mother, and from Kit. That would make sense: they loved their times in Hampstead. And that meant that the children must all move to London. Frieda would absolutely hate that idea too. I was relying on that.

Well then. Thinking it through, it would obviously be too much

lxx

to drag Maude and my parents up here to Nottingham, at their age: and I would also be too ashamed of the disaster of my marriage. The last thing I would have wanted to do was advertise to the town of Nottingham that I had no mother for my children because she had run off with a friend, so that I was obliged to go back to living with my parents. I could get myself a room somewhere near the College and the Victoria station.

This started off as a scheme to incite Frieda to come back. But it developed its own momentum. It was actually rather a good plan, even if Frieda came back. If the children were staying with my parents, I would have some hold over her, some bargaining power. So in fact the girls must now stay where they were, in Well Walk. And they must start going to school in London. Would they all fit in the house in Hampstead? For the moment, yes; though in the long run they would have to move. But we could cross that bridge when we came to it. Monty could stay with me here in Nottingham for the moment, until the end of the summer term. Then a London school for him too. I would work on in Nottingham, but then live in London and just be here in my lodgings in the week, for my teaching and other work. And – I was still sure – there would eventually come the move to the prestigious chair at Oxford or Cambridge, which would change everything; and the whole family could then come with me. And Frieda too. Perhaps.

All this became clear to me, just by pulling the thread which asked the question 'how do they get a mother?' And I knew all the time that it would actually take months to arrange all these things: that they were also threats, to try and make Frieda see what was imminently happening if she did not come back. To make her come back.

And then I think I dozed for an hour or so: to wake with another raging headache and a raging heart, too. Everything I had done for her! Everything I had given up! Sleeping with her had been the best time of my life: and I had had that taken away from me for no reason at all, except to allow her to go to bed with any ruffian she chose, and to lock me out of her life. Time after time: years and years of cold-hearted betrayal. She had told me after the birth

lxxi

of Barbara that she wanted to have a separate bedroom; and as we could afford a house which allowed it, she did. And from that point on, following Stafford's intervention and I thought kindly, even fatherly advice, I made love to Frieda only terribly rarely.

And all the time she was going great guns with Dowson, and Gross, and heaven knows who else besides: anyone who showed interest in her, presumably.

I scribbled another letter to her father on the Wednesday or Thursday, I forget which, just to bring him up to date with developments. I had no idea whether Frieda had been telling her people in Metz what was going on; I guessed not. I could queer that pitch, for sure. So I took my chance of doing so:

> Dear Papa!
> I am afraid that I need to tell you that all is over between Frieda and me. She herself must tell you the reasons, if you really wish to know them. I have no desire to write them down: you must trust me to say that they are really criminal, and of a kind which you yourself would never forgive in a woman with whom you were in any way connected. I am very sorry indeed to report this to a loving and trusting father, who has always treated me with fond respect, but I must explain where truth and justice lie. I am arranging for the children to live in London.
> Your loving son
> Ernst

What I subsequently learned, from letters from the Baronin, was that the family had already become aware of oddities in Frieda's behaviour – she had apparently introduced a man into the von Richthofen family home who had revealed himself no gentleman, and who had had to be shewn the door – and after cross-questioning her, her father had come profoundly to suspect what lay behind his daughter's behaviour. That was apparently the person she was with – of whose identity, if he were *not* Dowson –

lxxii

which he ought to be – I had as yet no idea. There was in my mind no doubt that, as Bickerstaff puts it, if he were a gentleman, he should fight me and if he were a scrub, I would horsewhip him. Or at least I would pursue him through the courts for damages and ruin him. But Papa was not entirely surprised to get my first note, therefore, and answered it in a loving little letter.

> My dear Ernst
> Frieda is behaving disgracefully; I always thought she had more sense. I deeply sympathise with you and can only say that – whatever happens – I hope you will go on knowing us and visiting us; it has been and always will be a pleasure having you as a son-in-law. Frieda really seems to be in an absurdly depraved state, and I am very, very sorry for you and your children. I am really inconsolable.
> You will be glad to hear that we have at least got rid of the man: packed him off to Trier. My daughter Else helped him believe that he was in danger of shortly being arrested; like an idiot, he had got his name taken by the military people here, but that was actually helpful in getting him out of town.
> With sympathetic and loving greetings
> Papa

I was already thoroughly regretting writing to him about what I had called criminal behaviour (I was thinking of the English legal phrase 'criminal conversation', meaning unlicensed sex) and had even termed disgusting – too much for a father to take, perhaps, and not really anything of which a son-in-law should complain. And I felt that I had revealed to him all my weaknesses. I wrote to him again on the Saturday:

> Dear Papa!
> Many thanks for your friendly letter. Against fate one can do nothing and we must all have patience with one another. I would only like to beg your

lxxiii

forgiveness for the frantic letters I wrote to you. I know you will forgive such a tortured man for so doing. Ten days long I was out of my mind. Yesterday was the climax and I was really not responsible. You see, I had to bear everything alone and the mind is as if gone. Tonight I have finally slept, the pressure is somewhat gone from my head and I am a human being again. Say that you forgive me. I am now trying to make plans for the future. We must see that we save something from such a shipwreck. If only I had retained my self-control to the end!

your loving son
Ernst.

Do not be inconsolable. Frieda is young and I hope that she will have only happiness in the future.

But by the time I wrote that, everything had changed yet again. I had discovered what had happened: I had learned what Frieda had been doing. Lawrence had written to me.

CHAPTER XV

What confronted me on the breakfast table on Friday 10 May –
only a week and a day after she had gone! – were two letters from
Metz: and I seized on the one with the handwriting I knew,
Frieda's own. I saw immediately that she was now trying to
backtrack on her 'Ganz Recent' of three days earlier. More than
once she used the word 'compromise', she asked what would be
best for the children, and she succeeded in not mentioning her
lover once. She did not mention money either, which must in fact
have been high on her list of priorities (though with both her
sisters there, it was possible they were helping her). But the
language was not her language; her family had clearly closed
ranks behind her and had coached her into writing as she now did.
The letter could in fact have been dictated to her by the clever
Else.

> Dear Ernst
> We are nearly thirteen years married, we love our
> children, and we cannot end our marriage in such a
> way. There must be some room for compromise in
> this horrible situation; you will agree with me that
> above all we must do what is best for the children.
> Would you please spell out to me the terms on
> which you would be prepared to continue as my
> husband, and what kind of compromise would be
> necessary to achieve that end. Just to state 'no
> possibility' is not only unhelpful but makes no
> provision for what will safeguard our children's
> future.
>   F.

At this point I had no idea that I also had a letter from Lawrence
on the breakfast table: a letter addressed in an unknown hand, and
also from Metz. I opened it unthinkingly, while planning my
answer to Frieda, imagining that it was a bill from a dressmaker,
or some such. It turned out to be a whining, blustering, at times

utterly incoherent confession of guilt – except that he swerved away at the end, to declare that he did not think, after all, that he was doing anything wrong. The impudence of it (it was his word, and it was right).

> You will know by now the extent of the trouble. Don't curse my impudence in writing to you. In this hour we are only simple men, and Mrs. Weekley will have told you everything, but you do not suffer alone. It is really torture to me in this position. There are three of us, though I do not compare my sufferings with what yours must be, and I am here as a distant friend, and you can imagine the thousand baffling lies it all entails. Mrs. Weekley hates it, but it has had to be. I love your wife and she loves me. I am not frivolous or impertinent. Mrs. Weekley is afraid of being stunted and not allowed to grow, and so she must live her own life. All women in their natures are like giantesses. They will break through everything and go on with their own lives. The position is one of torture for us all. Do not think I am a student of your class — a young cripple. In this matter are we not simple men? However you think of me, the situation still remains. I almost burst my heart in trying to think what will be best. At any rate we ought to be fair to ourselves. Mrs. Weekley must live largely and abundantly. It is her nature. To me it means the future. I feel as if my effort of life was all for her. Cannot we all forgive something? It is not too much to ask. Certainly if there is any real wrong being done I am doing it, but I think there is not.

> D. H. Lawrence

So it was not Dowson after all: but she had said 'Ganz Recent'. Could it be that she was having affairs with two men simultaneously? Knowing what I now knew, I wouldn't have put it past her. And here was that chuckle-head Lawrence saying that making love to my wife was a kind of torture. Well, that was some comfort (perhaps it had been the agonies of loving her which had turned him into that 'young cripple'? I could not understand anything in that part of his letter). But he was clearly getting on terribly badly with the von Richthofens, being only a 'distant friend' and having to tell all those baffling lies; and, what was more, I knew that they had had him kicked out of Metz, something of which – of course – he failed to inform me.

And to think of poor little Frieda as a giantess, being obliged to live largely and abundantly! She had, indeed, recently put on weight, as I had noted. But, assuming that he was *not* thinking of Baudelaire,[5] as I am perfectly sure he was not, how on earth could she have allowed this speculating, fantasising idiot near her? He was not in the least handsome – that was something to which I could testify, he was scrawny and obviously ill – and he was clearly incapable of stringing together two coherent sentences. His letter was simply a congeries of ideas. I later heard from her that he was 'very upsettable', which made me think that she had perhaps taken him on out of pity and have got stuck with him (she never could manage things like that sensibly: I thought of one or two men who had come knocking at our door begging, and how she had never had the nous to get rid of them).

But she had made her bed, and must lie in it. I wondered how long friend Lawrence would survive in it, though I also hated the thought of him being there. Only a week or two, I estimated; it might even be all over by now, with him packed off out of Metz. And then – was Dowson going to emerge? Was *he* standing in the wings waiting? Or was Lawrence her only lover? Was it possible he did not even know about Dowson? I later ensured that he did, the hard way, be passing on to him a note from Dowson which Frieda was idiotic enough to have left in a book she sent me: the note said 'why didn't you elope with me instead?' or something like that. Just enough to remind friend Lawrence that he was not

[5] Cf. 'La Géante' (*Fleurs du Mal*).

PROOFS EW ARWW 5-6 Feb.1939

the only man in Frieda's sights.

I wanted to hurt her. When she came back to Nottingham – I was now sure she would come back, driven if nothing else by desperate poverty and a dawning realisation of just how foolish she had been, risking all these men as her lovers, but also wanting her children back – then I would threaten her with the idea that she would never see them again and that she was also in danger of never getting a penny from me. Let her face having to rely on the financial support of her hopeless old father, gambling his life away, and see how she enjoyed that. I was not going to let her get away with her newly found tone of sweet, even loving reasonableness (I was more sure than ever that her family had been talking her into trying to be sensible) – and let her have it. I seized my pen and wrote her a stinker. I even failed to write 'Dear Frieda'. She was not a dear, not the shred of one, anymore. She had lied and lied and lied. Now was the moment to nail her lies to the counter.

I simply stated my new plans as things unchangeable, not as things to be discussed: I treated her as someone who no longer mattered in the larger scheme of things, but who might at times incidentally be helpful or useful.

> Do you want to drive me to suicide to simplify things? I will not do it. I shall write to or see the Hampstead people to-day. I am quite clear what I ought to do, but you ought to help me. The children will never come back to Nottingham. I shall take a house somewhere outside London – get the old people and Maud to move to it – they will do this for me – and I shall live between there and Nm as Oswald does. The children will go to school in London and form new friendships, and there will be a family home.

A family home which had no place for her in it: that was what I meant. And then I found myself saying straight out what I really thought:

lxxviii

All compromises are unthinkable. We are not
rabbits –

All this unlicensed sex, animal-like running from one man to
another: she was a rabbit, if anyone ever was. But I was at that
stage still weak enough to plead with her and ask for her help. The
alter Arsch that I was – she was right there!

> Do not let all generosity be on my side. Have some
> remorse for all your deception of a loving man. Let
> me know at once that you agree to a divorce – The
> thing can be managed very quietly, but unless you
> help by an admission, this will be difficult. And then
> it might cost me my post here and our children could
> starve. You loved me once – help me now – but
> quickly.   E

I remember how my hand trembled as I wrote that. I was, indeed,
beginning to be very scared about how the University might react
to a public scandal: I would only go ahead with a divorce (after
all, she ought in the end to be obliged to marry the man, however
much of a miserable worm he was) if it could all be kept
reasonably quiet. But I needed professional advice about my own
status and my future at the College. Later that day I dropped a note
to my splendid law colleague Dr Tinsley Lindley, asking if I might
call round during the weekend for a chat.

I also called Ida in and asked her to take my letter to catch the
10.15 a.m. collection. I wanted Frieda to get it as soon as possible.

I learned a great deal from Lawrence's letter: much more than
he probably thought. It was an extremely stupid letter for him to
have written, in fact, though damned useful to me when I had to
get the divorce through, a year and a half later. His letter did the
job as evidence beautifully. I also instructed my lawyer to feed the
letter to the press and they took the bait: I hoped they would make
so much of it that they would forget to publicise me. That did not
happen, unfortunately, though as a result of it friend Lawrence
must have come in for a good deal more publicity than he had ever

lxxix

expected. That preaching parson of a brother of his, George, must have been impressed and I hope a few dovecots in Eastwood were fluttered, though apparently he never *had* been a favourite son, back there.

He incidentally took his revenge on me by never paying the bill for costs which I had him sent, but at least that got him declared bankrupt; and I am sure his reputation as not just morally unsound but also as a bankrupt encouraged the authorities to act against him in 1915, when that slimy absurdity *The Rainbow* was published. But that is to run the story too far ahead.

Having sent that letter off, I felt better; and actually went in to the College for a couple of hours. But it was while walking home (walking to clear my head) that I realised a problem. I had declared that 'all compromises are unthinkable'. That was just the kind of sentence which, in the hands of an astute lawyer acting against me, might prove me to be unreasonable. I stopped at the Post Office at the bottom of the hill and sent a telegram saying that my letter to F. was not to be opened. I could always pretend that it should not be opened because its language was so violent (though I was very fond of my declaration 'we are not rabbits', made to someone who would clearly sleep with – or, to sling the bat at it, to fuck – any man she found). I would have gone all the way with Lord Fisher's 1919 remark (I quoted it in one of my dictionaries, thinking of Frieda as I did so) that that 'damned word "compromise"' was 'the beastliest word in the English language'. I would certainly not accept it from Frieda at such a moment, though I never forgot how she had used it: presumably to assure me that she would limit herself to three lovers a year, if I would promise to do the same, or something along those lines.

I slept a little that night, too. The next day came that sweet letter from her old father – also doing his best to ensure that I stayed within the fold. My support for Frieda, coupled I may confess with the occasional little bit of financial generosity towards him, were altogether too useful, what with the beautiful Johanna married to a gambler, and the spitefully clever Else married to an unsuccessful academic. And Frieda had just thrown in her lot with a man without any income at all, just occasional small lump sums

lxxx

if he were lucky with a publisher that year. The Baron certainly could not face having Frieda back on his hands.

But I was not out of the wood yet: not by any means. I could dash off these letters, sounding strong: and then I would dissolve into floods of tears again, or be filled with thoughts of violence; or sometimes just relapse into thoughts of her in bed, and wanting her, very very badly. There was one thing I could do, though; and I wanted to do it, and I did it. That same Friday evening I called in Ida and told her that I was very sorry, but that my wife would be staying in Germany for the foreseeable future (I offered no explanations), and that the children would be going to live with my parents in London: so that unfortunately, from the end of the month I would no longer have any need for her services. I said I would pay her wages up until the end of September, thus covering four months from the date of her dismissal. She had obviously been aware that – with all these telegrams – something was going on, but this sudden action, I could see, shocked her. But there was nothing she could do. She said she would leave at the end of the month (that is, the end of May), and I agreed that that would be best; she wanted in the meanwhile to try and get a job as Kindermädchen elsewhere in Nottingham and asked me if I would write her a reference. I said yes.

I had never liked her much. For one thing, she was terribly religious, and I was a little worried about her influence on the children and how it might make them pious. I wanted them God-fearing but not Pope-fearing. But for another thing it was clear that she and Frieda had grown very close; and as I couldn't get at Frieda at the moment, I wanted to hurt anyone who was close to her. Packing Ida off – it seemed to me unlikely that she would want another job in Nottingham, after her experience with the Flersheims, so that she would be unlikely to see Frieda again, and Frieda could never see her again without spending time and effort – and money which she did not have, and which I did not intend her to have – was an idea which actually satisfied me. I also called in Bertha and told her that I would not want her services after 1 August but that I would be grateful if she would not leave before that date.

lxxxi

And if Frieda came back, as I could still fantasise that she would, we would get a new nurse for the children – an English woman – who would not worm her way into Frieda's good books so easily. And another cook, not as friendly with Frieda either. For all my threats of immediate action, it actually suited me that for the moment I had only Monty to deal with, in Nottingham, the girls being taken care of in Hampstead. I could wait, I told myself, however much I would have liked to settle things at once. And who knows what might happen.

CHAPTER XVI

On the Monday the torrent of letters descended on me again. There were two more from Frieda; one she had written after getting my Friday letter, one written before, which was yet another influenced by her family (I could detect Else's hand in it, again) and begging for compromise.

But I couldn't have this: I just could not bear having the wound opened up again and again, just when I was starting to sleep once more. I scribbled off a letter to the Frau Baronin, demanding that someone shut Frieda up. I extensively exaggerated the degree to which I was being affected by her letters, I must admit. I confess that I was also trying to make Frieda sorry for me, in an effort to make her come back. I was also, for sure (I can now admit), a great deal afflicted with self-pity: and I also hinted at the raging violence that I found kept bursting out in me. But nothing like this had ever happened to me before, in my life.

> Dear Mama
> Today came two letters from Frieda, in one she talks of a compromise, in the second she says she will come and help me with the move. Dear Mama, please make her understand in what a state I am: I cannot see her handwriting without starting to tremble like an old paralytic – to see her again would be death to me. I would kill myself and the children too. It is terrible when one so longs for death and yet must live for others. I'm not killing myself, but she *has* to leave me in peace. She knows that she can depend upon my honour. Today I hoped that the rattling in my head had half disappeared, but these letters have taken my bit of good sense away again. She *must* leave everything to me, if only for practical reasons.

I thought it best to add in that line about *not* killing myself. But the bit about the rattling in my head was perfectly true; it was a

lxxxiii

kind of headache that shifted around, from which I had never suffered before, and which went on and on (I was still suffering from it six months later).

But I ended that letter, after a bit more self-pity, more resolved and certain, in a way which also constituted something of a threat:

> I will fight with my despair and find the best solution – She must understand that she has no more rights but she knows that I am decent.

Knowing Frieda as I did, I was perfectly sure that she would not understand any such concept as 'having no more rights' (would not actually understand what having rights meant, either: people of her background never considered the rights of others, only their own inviolable superiority of birth, and getting their own way). She would inevitably try to go on behaving exactly as she wanted to. But at least her mother had had that shot fired across her bows and knew the situation; and Frieda, without the Lawrence bloke in play any more (that at least was my hope), would very quickly come round and start begging to be taken back.

That constituted the end of what we might call Round One of the match. I had come out well ahead on points; but Frieda, although floored to the canvas more than once by what you might call knock-down arguments, had the habit (she had always had it) of simply getting up and coming back for more. As ever, she had no idea that she was down for the count, with her own arguments pulverised. She simply wanted what she wanted, and went on demanding it. I actually gloated at the way young Lawrence could have had no idea what kind of a woman (or family) he had taken on. She would drive him wild in double quick time, if they ever looked like staying together: and I guessed that by now they had gone separate ways (though I was wrong there).

PROOFS EW ARWW 5-6 Feb.1939

I now started the pretence of breaking up the household in Nottingham. The two girls were already in London: thank goodness for that. But what I could do was ensure that at least some of their things (clothes, boots, and dolls) were sent after them; and no-one could deal with such things better than Ida. I set her to work; and I made sure that Frieda heard what was happening. Monty could stay exactly as he was for the moment; we would do nothing else until the long vacation, by which time Frieda would probably be at the door, pleading with me – and we could come to some kind of agreement.

What secretly I most of all wanted – and I do not think she ever knew this – was to have my marital rights over her restored. During the last few months it had been made horribly clear to me that she was not capable of conceiving a child, no matter how many men she took as lovers; they cannot all have been impotent or infertile. Old Dr Stafford had clearly colluded with her in saying that another pregnancy would be dangerous for her; it was just that she wanted no more of me, having other men in her sights. Well, now – to put it very crudely – I wanted her back so that I could have her as often as I wanted, with the threat that I would kick her out on the streets if she did not comply. If truth be told, there was still a corner or more in me which hoped that she might come back of her own volition, and that we would find a way of living – if not exactly together in the full sense, then at least as neighbours, with sexual access. Living together, in the fullest sense, family and all, was probably impossible. Anyway, keeping the girls down in London for the moment, to strengthen my hand, was obviously sensible; she could only see them when I chose. But having her nearby, so that I could have her when I wanted (lovely word, 'have') – that was something which I still revengefully desired.

Following my letter to her mother, things went quiet for a while. It had not, however, taken me long to find out from Lindley (I saw him on the Tuesday) that a divorce could not be arranged quietly, even with Frieda's co-operation. The popular newspapers, he told

PROOFS EW ARWW 5-6 Feb.1939

me in confidence, watch the divorce courts like hawks, and write up anything that sounds the least bit juicy (I was not used to reading such newspapers); and a Professor losing his wife to a young writer, I was assured, would be just the kind of thing they would eagerly seize upon.

Right then, I thought. Why bother to divorce her? What would be the advantage? So that she could marry her coal-miner lover, who doubtless dreams of marrying into the aristocracy? I did not see why I should provide either her or him with that pleasure, possibly at the cost of my own career (though Lindley did not think there was much chance of that), but certainly at the cost of ignominy in Nottingham. Better to leave things as they were. It was not as if I wanted to marry anyone else.

I confess, this decision also pandered to my deepest desire – that she would come back. Why set out to divorce her when I actually wanted to remain married to her, every bedding of her a proof of my continuing marital rights and of what I hoped might be her new-found humility and submissiveness?

This policy, however, led to a summer and autumn of letters, and demands, and counter-demands, in which I must say I leant over backwards to be fair to her, eventually promising her access to the children in the spring of 1913 (by which time, I trusted, they would have forgotten all about her, which I would take pleasure in telling her). I linked this, however, with the demand that she leave Lawrence and return to live in England, at a place of my choosing. Being Frieda, she interpreted this as the promise of a flat of her own and access to the children when she came back in the spring; and she was desperately disappointed when that turned out not to be the case.

She also, astonishingly and absurdly, sent me a wadge of letters from Otto Gross: wild, impossible mad rants. They showed to me how unsteady was the basis on which she was now taking her stand; I knew her own 'bottom of good sense' (thank you, Dr Johnson) well enough to believe that she would not go on being impressed by such productions.

CHAPTER XVIII

I however decided, after months of such letters, from her and Gross and from the Lawrence lout, and no sign that she was coming back under her own steam (she was back again with Lawrence, down in Italy) that enough was enough. I had been pretty insulting, I fear, promising for example to hand her over to the police when as a prostitute she accosted me in Piccadilly Circus, after her failure with Lawrence. But finally I realised, around Christmas 1912, that I was going to have to divorce her. This was profoundly irritating, but there was nothing else I could reasonably do to ensure that I kept control over the children.

For I had been assured that in my particular case a divorce court would be sure to award me legal custody of the children and that Frieda would have no further right to see them until they were each twenty-one years old. I had been to see the German Consul in the Ropewalk, to see if he could shed any light on the legal status within Germany of any decision about child custody taken in Great Britain; he could not (though I ensured that Frieda heard about this, hoping that it would scare her somewhat). But the solicitor recommended to me by Lindley, Charles Rothera, was perfectly certain that the only sure way of ensuring my future custody of the children would be for me to divorce Frieda and have the children legally settled on me. I took some months thinking this over. But it was what I eventually opted, still with great reluctance, to do. I deeply hated the thought of the publicity.

I wrote to Frieda, therefore, in January 1913, that I had done with her and that I wished to forget her (not true: but it had to be said). I turned the knife by adding that she in turn must be dead to the children: 'You know that the law is on my side.' My communications with her perforce ceased; and I confess that, out of sheer emotional exhaustion, I was more than happy for this period to commence, however wretched it also made me.

But Rothera had counselled me that, for the sake of evidence in court, it would be best to provide some proof that Frieda was indeed committing adultery with Lawrence; and given that by December she was living on Lake Garda, at first it looked a very

lxxxvii

difficult matter to ensure that proof of the requisite kind could be established. Again, assurance was given that evidence of their living in the same flat would be sufficient; and in this situation I was utterly indebted to the courage and independence of my sister Maude, who offered to travel to Italy and establish the facts as far as she could. She had, fortunately, a little German (ironically, during one summer holiday when I was away she had learned it from Frieda in Hampstead!) And a Baedeker showed me that Gargnano had at least two German hotel keepers (or hotel keepers' wives).

Maude set off on this extraordinary journey at the start of January 1913; it was possible for her to get a series of trains to the port of Riva, and then to take the boat down to Gargnano. Even with sleeper accommodation, this was a long, difficult and exhausting journey; but Maude managed it. She made contact with the Hotel Gargnano, just by the port, which fortunately turned out *not* to be the hotel where Frieda and Lawrence had made friends with the hotel-owner's wife, Frau Samuelli. But this other lady also knew all about the English man and the German woman who lived together in the house of Pietro di Paoli; and Maude having arranged to stay at the hotel, the woman actually escorted her to the Villa Igea – where by the greatest stroke of good fortune, she actually saw Frieda and Lawrence together, leaving the house. Maude had been perfectly prepared to knock on the door of the Villa Igea herself, but that proved unnecessary; what she managed to do was talk secretly to Maria Samuelli and to establish that there was no doubt at all that Frieda had since the end of September been living with Lawrence in a flat in that building. The names of Maria Samuelli and of the owner of the accommodation, Pietro di Paoli, were established, and statements were drafted by both of them. And Maude was able to return with these precious documents without, I believe, Frieda or Lawrence ever having become aware that she had been in Gargnano.

PROOFS EW ARWW 5-6 Feb.1939

CHAPTER XIX

In the summer of 1913, however, back in England, Frieda started things all over again. What I should have anticipated, had I thought ahead, was that she might go to St Paul's School to waylay Monty. And that is what she did, pretending to be an aunt who wanted to see him. According to his later confession, she got him out of school for an hour and stuffed him with cakes and cream, as well as handing over half a crown for him and the others. He also became the bearer of a note to the girls which attempted to get them to ask to see her. Fortunately, Maude found the note and then discovered the half crown.

Frieda was also observed, from the upstairs windows of the Chiswick house, standing outside in the rain under a tree, but with her hat and clothes already soaked, until she went away of her own volition. Her next attempt was simply to watch for the children when they left for school, and attempt to stop them in the street. Fortunately I was prepared for this and had arranged with Maude that, for the next few weeks, she or one of her sisters would always accompany the children down the street when they left; and when, on one occasion, my sister Kit saw the figure of Frieda bearing down, she was able to shout 'Run, run, children!' so that they could get away before Frieda could stop them. But before I even knew this, I had decided that serious action must be taken, and I went to the trouble of obtaining a court order forbidding her from interfering with the children; and I had this delivered to the only address I securely had for her and Lawrence, that of the *outré* literary gentleman Edward Garnett, down in Kent (she had written from that address on first getting back to England in June).

I also wrote to her, via her mother (until the divorce was through, I could not write directly) declaring that she was now – or should be – dead to the children, she being no more than a decaying corpse (*eine verfaulte Leiche*) to them. An extremely unpleasant image, to be sure, but no more than the truth. I wished to convey to her not just how utterly remote from them she now was, but what a frightening, alien, even disgusting being she had become. I believed at least that this was true; it was certainly true

lxxxix

of Elsa, perhaps of Monty. Of Barbara I was not sure; I recall her telling me, years later, that life had always been such fun when Frieda had been there: 'wonderful, magical', she said. It obviously took time for such feelings to die.

CHAPTER XX

The hearing was scheduled for October 1913, and everything went as smoothly as might have been expected, given that the divorce was unopposed. I had half wondered if she would appear, but she did not. The whole thing, in court, took only about fifteen minutes. I had first consulted with Rothera about the ways in which publicity about the case might be minimised, but he had warned me that any attempt to buy off any segment of the newspaper industry would simply create a vortex of interest on the part of the industry not so suborned – and presumably I could not afford to bribe everyone to remain silent. I went to my London solicitors (Templeton and Barrett) with the same question; but they unfortunately returned the same answer. Templeton thought, however, that my idea of releasing the relevant text of Lawrence's letter to the Press was a good one, and assisted in making carbon copies of it which could be handed out, in an attempt to direct the Press's interest away from me, and at least damaging Lawrence, so far as I could. Templeton also happened to be an old friend of the legal correspondent of the *Times*, who promised to do what he could to ensure that there, at least, only a minimal account of the proceedings would be printed.

There was a brief report in the *Evening Standard* the evening of the hearing, a Friday (I was still in London after the hearing, and saw the paper), but I hoped that would go unnoticed. What sank me and my hopes was the fact that there was nothing else sensational on offer to the Press that particular weekend. A juicy case of bigamy or a horrid murder would have assisted me greatly. As a result, a long report appeared in the *Nottinghamshire Guardian* on the Saturday – fatal for my situation in Nottingham, as I discovered when I got back there on the Sunday, and was told by various friends what had happened. But more lasting damage was probably done to me by the appearance in the Sunday *News of the World* of a piece on the front page. Templeton passed this on to me and I still have it, as a grim relic of what sank my career. My case had offered the correspondent of the *News of the World* his best chance of a splash – and he took it gratefully. It made, as

xci

a result, what one might accurately term *a terrific scandal*.

The effect on the worthies at Nottingham I never heard at first hand, but various rumours reached me. I was told that principal Heaton took my part (which was just as well) but also that a number of my colleagues chose to sign a joint letter to him demanding that the College do what it could to counter the terrible publicity generated by the public exposure of misbehaviour touching the College so nearly. That was a polite way of saying 'get rid of him'. I kept my job and my chair but all prospects of promotion within the College were ruled out, in spite of the fact that I was becoming (and eventually became) a far better known and far more prestigious figure than anyone else at the College, Stanley Kipping excepted. One senior figure almost gave the game away a few years later when, at a gathering of figures from the past, brought together to meet the younger generation, I heard this peevish old voice saying 'that bounder Weekley: why in heaven's name did they not take the advice of the Senate and sack him?' He was then hushed into inaudibility by the person to whom he was talking, who had seen me nearby. But I had heard enough. So *that* had happened in Senate, had it? Doubtless at one of the meetings I had been unable to attend, because of going to see my legal representatives in London, in the autumn of 1913. Well, I stayed on. But that was my career *up the spout* (from, of course, the pawnbroker's lift for pledged articles).

The worst episode, by far, however, came eight months later, in the summer of 1914, when Frieda actually succeeded in getting into the Chiswick house one evening. I was not there, which was probably just as well. She would have guessed that the children usually had their tea at five o'clock; accordingly, just before five she slipped round the side of the house, and got in the unlocked back door; and then, by instinct, made her way to the ground floor kitchen where indeed the children were just starting their tea. Luckily neither of my parents was present but Kit told me all about it. Frieda just walked in, calling out the children's names, clearly expecting them to run to her and embrace her. In fact only Barbara made any attempt to do this. Elsa actually got up and ran to the other side of the room, Monty just stood up and said and did

xcii

nothing. Kit pounced on Barbara and pulled her away from Frieda and dragged her to the other side of the room, getting kicked in the process. Frieda was just left standing; and Elsa started to shout 'Get out, get out, you are not our mother, we don't want you here.' Monty stayed silent but looked white in the face. And then Kit went over to Frieda and told her to go. After a pause, and after looking at the children, Frieda did indeed allow herself to be shewn the door, taken out the back, taken to the front gate, and there left outside, with the gate bolted.

The children were terribly upset. They had at first regularly asked where she was, to which the standard reply had been 'Still in Germany'; and if they asked 'And when is she coming back?' the standard answer had been 'When she can'. But the episode of the note and the half crown the previous year, and then the chase in the street, had put paid to that version of events (Monty had also doubtless told his sisters about the time when she had found him in St Paul's). The attempt had then been made never to refer to her in any way, in the family home, and to answer any queries with the formula 'you must talk to your father about that' – and I remained unforthcoming. But then came the episode in the kitchen at the children's tea. Kit, very sensibly, made no comments about what had just happened, just ensured that the children went on with their tea (only Barbara objected and refused to eat any more).

I later learned that the children had decided, between themselves, sometime between the summer of 1913 and the summer of 1914, that their mother had been confined to a lunatic asylum, and occasionally escaped, which was why sometimes she just turned up, out of the blue; and that was why running away from her or ignoring her was the best thing to do, even if she pleaded with them. This was obviously an excellent thing, as it accounted both for her sudden and unexpected arrivals and the fact they had best not go near her. We were happy to let this version of events prevail; and together (I am for ever grateful to my mother for taking on this extra duty, in her old age) we did our very best to give the children as normal, as disciplined and as loving an upbringing as possible.

At Christmas 1914, however, clearly emboldened by the way

xciii

she had got into the Chiswick house in the summer, Frieda also managed to see me in Nottingham one evening by giving a false name at the front door. Miss Ryker mistakenly showed her in. Her hair was badly dressed, she looked much older; the whole experience was shocking. As soon as I could interrupt her torrent of demands to see the children, I simply told her the truth: that the children themselves not only wished to have nothing more to do with her, but that legally she had no right to approach them, and that she risked arrest if she did. I also told her that I perfectly understood the children's reluctance to have anything to do with her, as she had sufficiently distanced them by preferring the sexual enticements of someone not even a *gentleman* to being their mother, and could as a result hardly expect to be treated *as* a mother. She said, monotonously, over and over, that she simply wanted to see the children, though she also announced that she and Lawrence were now married. All I could do was ring for Miss Ryker and have her shewn out.

It had nevertheless been a terribly upsetting event; and she *was*, after all, now married (I checked up on that). I began to think that a simple official meeting with the children, at which they could say what they felt, but in the presence of my legal representatives, might be a way of bringing this series of desperate, absurd and upsetting confrontations to an end. Accordingly, when she wrote to me again the following summer, I decided to give her an unexpected birthday surprise (I never forget the day) though also, I hoped, a shock by summoning her to my London solicitors in August 1915, bringing the children there myself by taxi, and then leaving them together for exactly thirty minutes, with Templeton present to intervene if anything untoward occurred. Afterwards I and the children were driven back to Chiswick. It was a very silent journey, I remember, but I did not want to initiate any conversation or any revelations. Monty simply asked me whether I knew that Mama was now married again, and I told him that I did know it, but that I did not think her new husband was the kind of person with whom they ought to associate. And there the conversation lapsed.

She was in London again in September 1916 and begged me to be allowed to see the children; and it turned out that they *would*, in spite of everything, like to see her. So I again permitted her half an hour with them, this time in the studio of the artist Mark Gertler, whom we had got to know in Hampstead back in 1911. These meetings seemed to do the children no harm, and I allowed one – or was it two – more of them – until, in the autumn of 1919, Frieda decided to go to Germany to see her relations . . . a journey which somehow took her round the world as well, and from which she returned only in September 1923, according to Monty, who (then being over twenty-one) at that point chose to see her; while she also attempted to see Elsa, who for the moment rebuffed her requests.

There then followed a rather disgraceful episode in England in 1925, when she tried to persuade Barby (not yet twenty-one) to stay overnight, out in Pentrich, with her and Lawrence, against the specific demands of the Kipping family, with whom Barby was staying in Nottingham (I was away at the time); and Mrs Kipping had to threaten to come out to Pentrich to rescue Barby before Frieda would give up on her persuasions. After that I was careful in cautioning Barby to lodge no closer than Alassio when visiting Frieda on the Italian Riviera: Frieda was in Spotorno. In fact, in this case Frieda's manipulative wiles won out; in October, Barby had her twenty-first birthday, and Frieda and Lawrence had her to stay in Spotorno over Christmas. And it must have been then that she talked at such length and in such coarse detail about her upbringing, and her grandmother, and about me. There is a revealing detail in the *Virgin and the Gipsy* about the abandoned vicar remembering his departed wife in his will. That was something which Barbara must actually have heard me mention, as something I had once done. I had reckoned that Frieda might have to play some part in taking care of her daughters if my parents were to die, and I were to die young, which at one stage had seemed more than likely (I had felt sure I was going mad, and that the children would be left fatherless). And she would then need finance to do the job properly. I had left my will like that, its details happily forgotten, even after the children had reached their twenty-first birthdays. But as soon as I read the story, I remembered – and had the will changed. She gets nothing from me, ever.

CHAPTER XXI

I heard no more directly of Frieda though I seemed to go on learning a lot about her from coming across reviews of Lawrence's work, and reading about his various heroines, as the books streamed out over the years. He never seems to have invented anything, which I would have deemed a limitation in a creative artist; but, as a result, at least I became acquainted with where Frieda and he had been going. In 1913 they had been in Italy and – after the War – in Sicily; and then in the 1920s they had travelled to Australia, and so to New Mexico, finally to Mexico itself. And then they were back in Europe, as demonstrated by my daughters' encounters with them.

Over the long years from 1913, down to my retirement in 1937, I never knew for certain what the effect of my divorce had been on the members of the senior common rooms in Oxford and Cambridge. But I could guess. No invitation to apply for a chair there was ever forthcoming. It was I, not they, who counted as soiled goods (academics as a body of people were once very justly characterised as scholasticall squitter-bookes). There are various entries in my *Etymological Dictionary* suggestive of my feelings: where 'College' is for example defined as 'community . . . in ref. to Oxf. and Camb.', but I spend more time on '*College pudding*? for earlier *New College* (Oxf.) *pudding* (Landor)' than on either of the great old universities. I also refer sarcastically to the 'mod. sense of *university* being tinged with the idea of universal learning'. Enough said. Of that great work, the *Dictionary*, I remain proud: not many of those who get chairs in Oxford or Cambridge are singly responsible for a major dictionary, or are told by Jack Squire that 'It is a very great pleasure to get a dictionary from Mr. Weekley. One knows from experience that Mr. Weekley would contrive to avoid unnecessary dullness, even if he were compiling a railway guide, but that he would also get the trains right.' I believe I managed that, in my *Dictionary*: at least I got the etymological junctions, timings, links and connections right.

It would however be proper to end this brief narrative with the

xcvi

quotation which I employed at the end of the Preface I wrote for the *Dictionary*: 'I force myself to laugh at everything, for fear of being obliged to weep over it'. My feelings then had been those forced to the surface by that terrible War; but my levity, I know, was and is a means of defence, for ever and a day. It has been my main standby in adversity since 1912. But with imagination of a new war crowding out so many other feelings, and in terrible consciousness of how age assaults us, so that our pretty plumage fades, the proud, billiard-brilliant and sexually aroused body droops and weakens, loses its faculties, no longer responds, I wish here nonetheless to record that I do not forget her, and never will. 'So sad, so fresh, the days that are no more'. I wear my wedding ring still: I have not taken it off since the day she put it on my finger in August 1899. (I wonder what she did with the ring I gave to her? Lost it, probably.) In the back of my watch I still keep that little picture of us together on the seat at the *Eichberghaus*, and I am conscious of it every night when I lay my watch down. It calls out to me 'from forty years ago', as Hardy put it: he too knew how the past calls and how we yearn. And forty years it will be, this coming year.

I must say once and for all that, in spite of all the ways she behaved to me subsequently, my marriage to her remains the most marvellous experience of my life. And in spite of the tragedy of life from 1912 onwards, of which she was the sole cause, my love for and devotion to her remain the greatest experience I have ever had, or (as I am now certain) I ever shall have. Although I have in the past hated and hated her, and for years believed – with good reason, I think – that she had a heart of stone, I also trust that she had at least a partly decent life with Lawrence; and I feel for her now that he has been gone for so long, although I also feel confident that whatever she is now doing, there will be a man involved. That is the person she is; and for all the way she damaged me so terribly, and showed how little she cared either for morality or for decency, there is a corner in me which – in a fashion that I usually keep hidden from myself, and have largely excluded from this narrative – admires her. My mind so easily finds its way back to Molière: *Il faut, parmi le monde, une vertu traitable*. That, I never managed. Frieda always did, and enjoyed her life as a result, I believe.

But I am also still able, sadly, to promise her that, whatever has happened to her – and to me – since 1899, 'I am just the same as when / Our days were a joy, and our paths through flowers'. As I write that down, my memories of the heaps of flowers at our wedding in Freiburg (still beloved Freiburg) come flooding back – I had never encountered such flowers. And I see our dear Black Forest lying in sunshine; and I recall our joy, walking in the pinewoods and preparing for the lifetime before us. Thank you, dear Hardy, for reminding me – reminding us all – how we carry our own past with us, in spite of everything. Dear man, you wrote those words in 1912, my year of years, if no thanks to Frieda, only once dear. Let me end simply with that enigma (from, of course, αἰνίσσεσθαι, to speak obscurely: *Brevis esse laboro, Obscurus fio*).

ERNEST WEEKLEY.

NOTTINGHAM
January 1939.

UNCORRECTED SET.

Having produced this set of excellent proofs (without
the puritanical Scottish printers offering any kind
of objection, I note), my bloody publisher decides
not to ~~publish~~ accept the book unless I cut it heavily.
He declares it the filthiest (ha!) he has ever read. I
shall certainly not cut it for him. He also says that
he could not publish a book ending in Greek and
Latin, as if it were not possible even for an
uneducated person to work out that I work at
brevity, I grow obscure . . .

     Clodhopper. Enough said. E. W.

           2 Mar. '39

www.ingramcontent.com/pod-product-compliance
Lightning Source LLC
Chambersburg PA
CBHW032001170626
46807CB00006B/2594